toto
TROUBLE

Thierry Coppée • Story and Art
Lorien • Color

PAPERCUT*Z*

New York

*Thanks to Valérie, Théo and Julien for their
patience and support.
Thanks to Mich for his February message.
Thanks to Guy for his trust.
Thanks to Lorien for listening.
Thanks to Thierry for his work behind the scenes.*

To my parents and grandparents.

TOTO TROUBLE Graphic Novels
Available from Papercutz

Graphic Novel #1
"Back to Crass"

Coming Soon!
Graphic Novel #2
"A Deadly Jokester"

TOTO TROUBLE graphic novels are available for $7.99 in
paperback, and $12.99 in hardcover. Available from booksellers
everywhere. You can also order online from papercutz.com. Or call
1-800-886-1223, Monday through Friday, 9 – 5 EST. MC, Visa, and
AmEx accepted. To order by mail, please add $4.00 for postage
and handling for first book ordered, $1.00 for each additional book,
and make check payable to NBM Publishing. Send to: Papercutz,
160 Broadway, Suite 700, East Wing, New York, NY 10038.

papercutz.com

TOTO TROUBLE #1 "Back to Crass"
Les Blagues de Toto, volumes 1-2, Coppée
© Éditions Delcourt, 2003-2004

Thierry Coppée – Writer & Artist
Lorien – Colorist
Joe Johnson – Translation
Tom Orzechowski – Lettering
Michael Petranek – Associate Editor
Jim Salicrup
Editor-in-Chief

ISBN: 978-1-59707-726-2 paperback edition
ISBN: 978-1-59707-777-4 hardcover edition

Printed in China
April 2014 by New Era Printing LTD
Unit C, 8/F, Worldwide Centre
123 Tung Chau Street, Hong Kong

Papercutz books may be purchased for business or promotional use.
For information on bulk purchases please contact Macmillan Corporate and
Premium Sales Department at (800) 221-7945 x5442.

Distributed by Macmillan
First Papercutz Printing

"My Name is Toto"

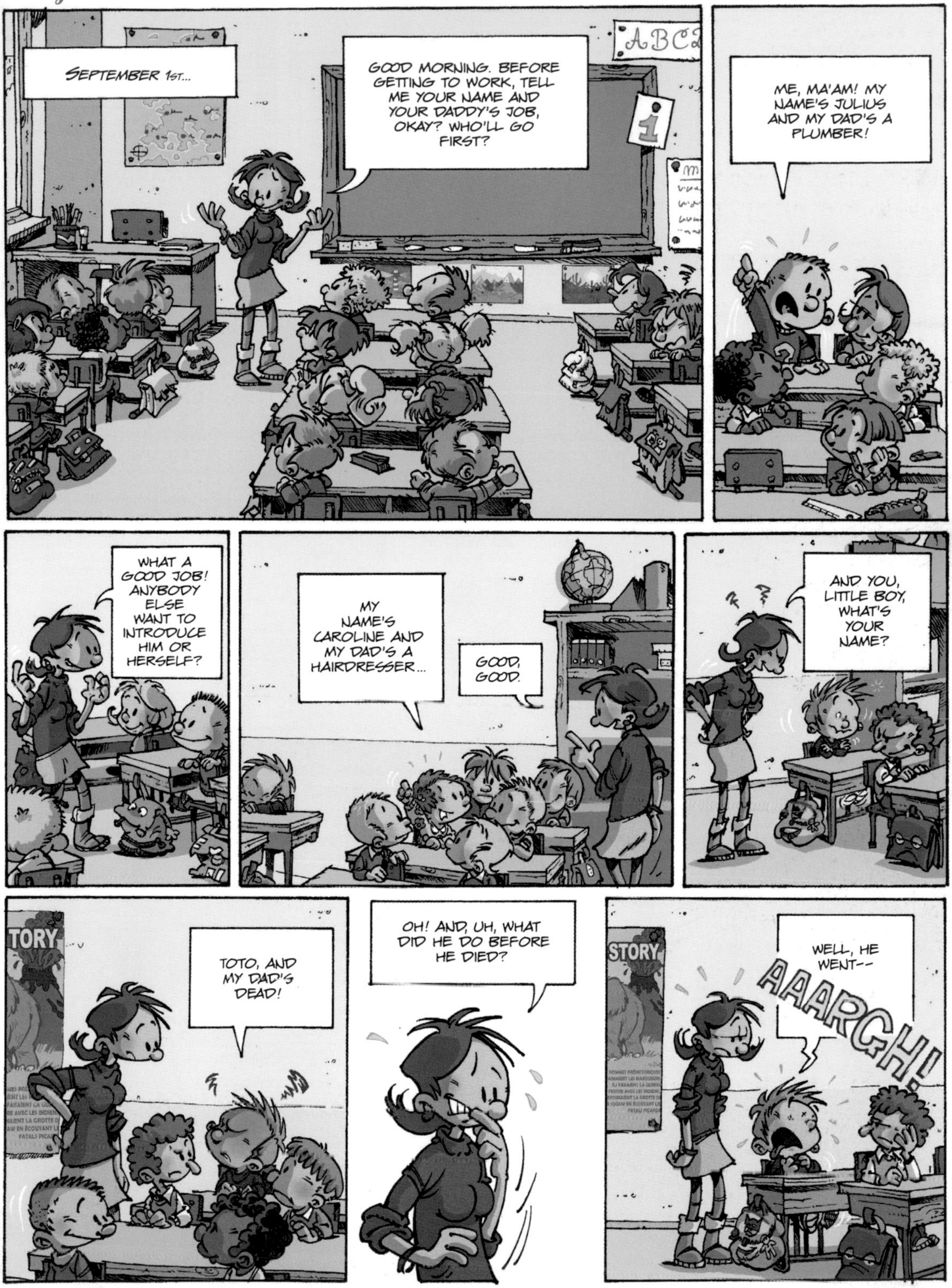
SEPTEMBER 1ST...
GOOD MORNING. BEFORE GETTING TO WORK, TELL ME YOUR NAME AND YOUR DADDY'S JOB, OKAY? WHO'LL GO FIRST?
ABC
ME, MA'AM! MY NAME'S JULIUS AND MY DAD'S A PLUMBER!
WHAT A GOOD JOB! ANYBODY ELSE WANT TO INTRODUCE HIM OR HERSELF?
MY NAME'S CAROLINE AND MY DAD'S A HAIRDRESSER...
GOOD, GOOD.
AND YOU, LITTLE BOY, WHAT'S YOUR NAME?
TORY
TOTO, AND MY DAD'S DEAD!
OH! AND, UH, WHAT DID HE DO BEFORE HE DIED?
STORY
WELL, HE WENT--
AAARGH!

"Thinking of You..."

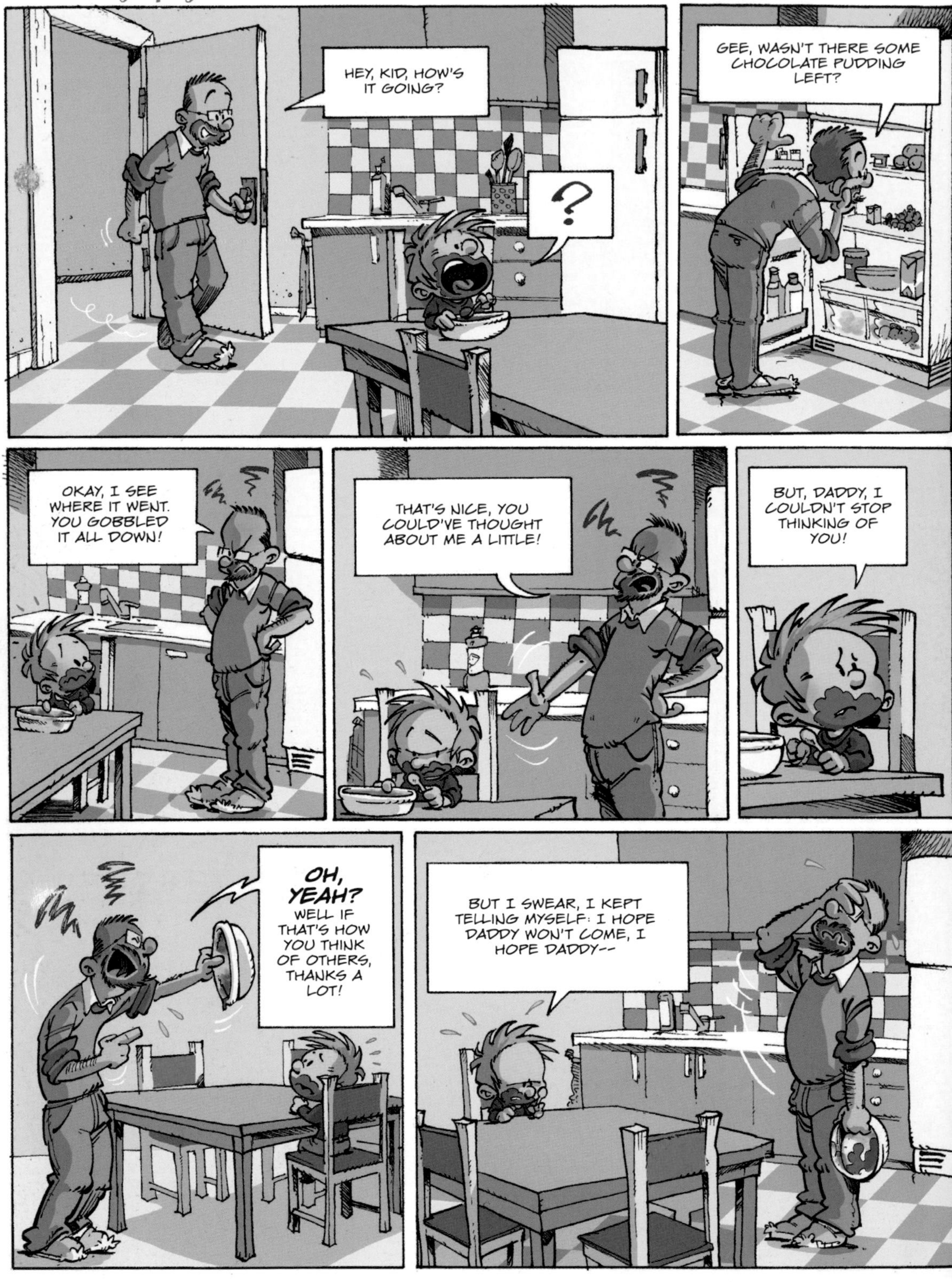
HEY, KID, HOW'S IT GOING?
?
GEE, WASN'T THERE SOME CHOCOLATE PUDDING LEFT?
OKAY, I SEE WHERE IT WENT. YOU GOBBLED IT ALL DOWN!
THAT'S NICE, YOU COULD'VE THOUGHT ABOUT ME A LITTLE!
BUT, DADDY, I COULDN'T STOP THINKING OF YOU!
OH, YEAH? WELL IF THAT'S HOW YOU THINK OF OTHERS, THANKS A LOT!
BUT I SWEAR, I KEPT TELLING MYSELF: I HOPE DADDY WON'T COME, I HOPE DADDY--

"Questions for a Champion-1"

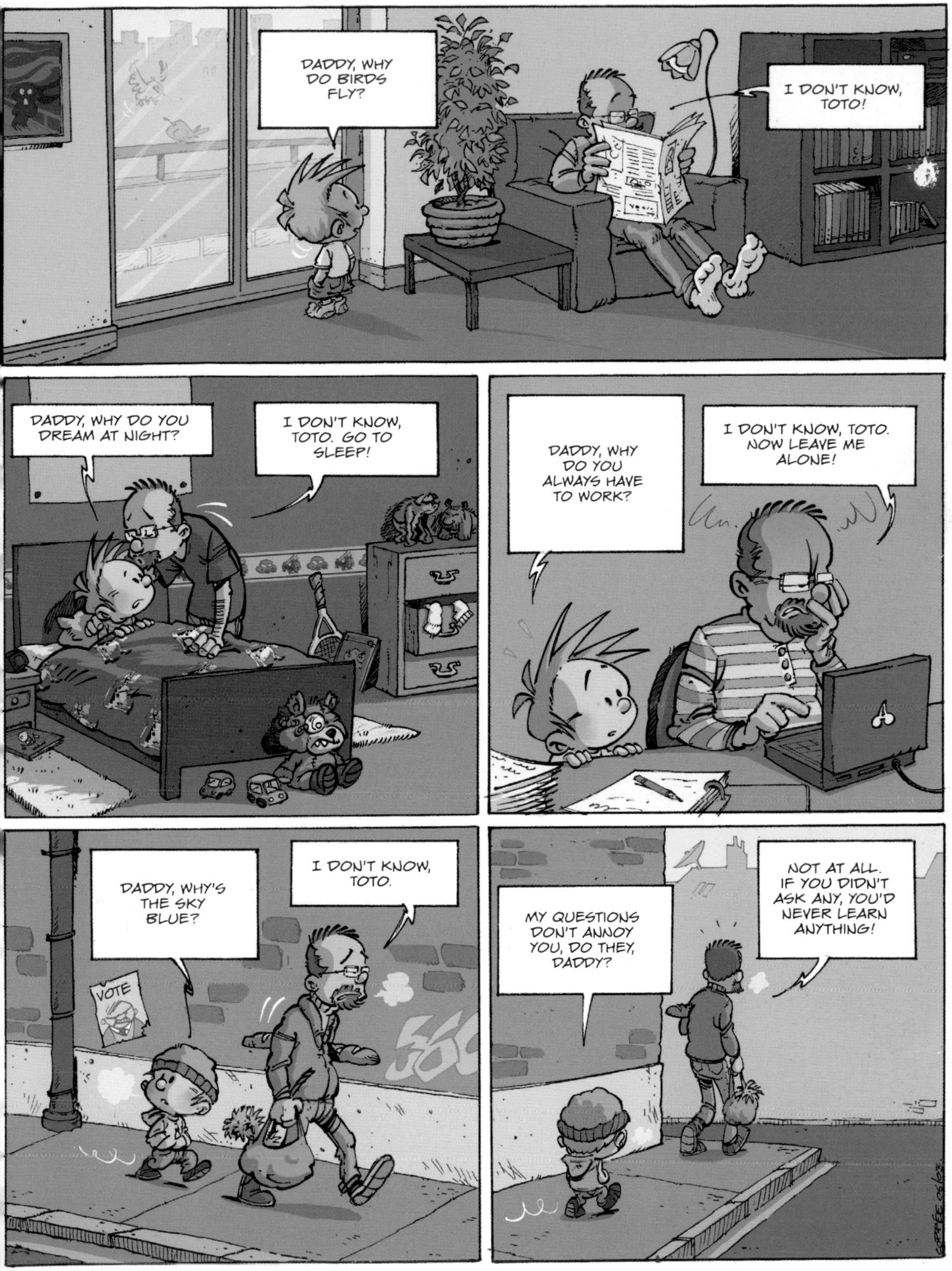

DADDY, WHY DO BIRDS FLY?
I DON'T KNOW, TOTO!
DADDY, WHY DO YOU DREAM AT NIGHT?
I DON'T KNOW, TOTO. GO TO SLEEP!
DADDY, WHY DO YOU ALWAYS HAVE TO WORK?
I DON'T KNOW, TOTO. NOW LEAVE ME ALONE!
DADDY, WHY'S THE SKY BLUE?
I DON'T KNOW, TOTO.
VOTE
MY QUESTIONS DON'T ANNOY YOU, DO THEY, DADDY?
NOT AT ALL. IF YOU DIDN'T ASK ANY, YOU'D NEVER LEARN ANYTHING!

"I Love You, But..."

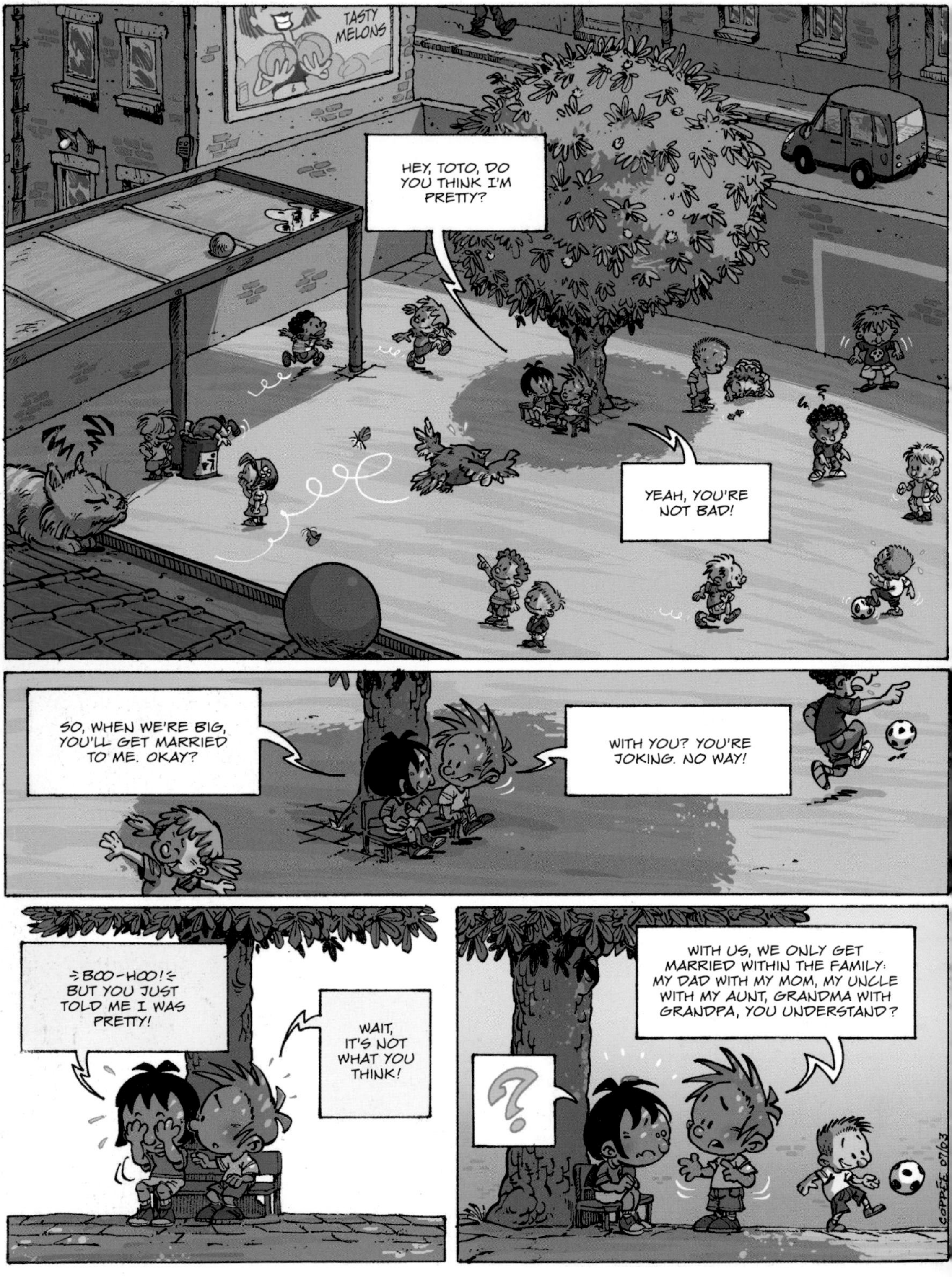
TASTY MELONS
HEY, TOTO, DO YOU THINK I'M PRETTY?
YEAH, YOU'RE NOT BAD!
SO, WHEN WE'RE BIG, YOU'LL GET MARRIED TO ME. OKAY?
WITH YOU? YOU'RE JOKING. NO WAY!
≈BOO-HOO!≈ BUT YOU JUST TOLD ME I WAS PRETTY!
WAIT, IT'S NOT WHAT YOU THINK!
?
WITH US, WE ONLY GET MARRIED WITHIN THE FAMILY: MY DAD WITH MY MOM, MY UNCLE WITH MY AUNT, GRANDMA WITH GRANDPA, YOU UNDERSTAND?
COPPÉE 07/03

"Hamming It Up"

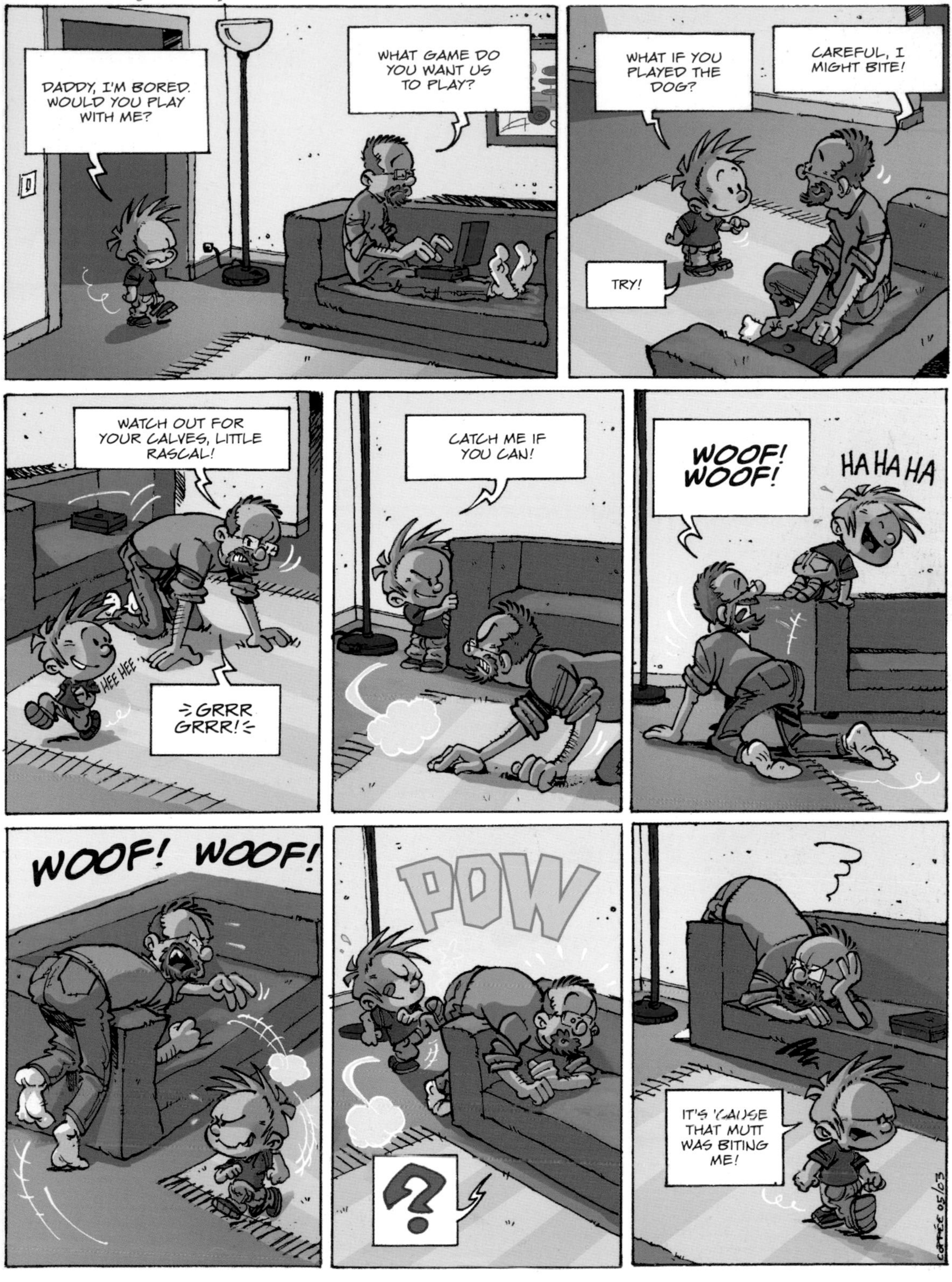
DADDY, I'M BORED. WOULD YOU PLAY WITH ME?
WHAT GAME DO YOU WANT US TO PLAY?
WHAT IF YOU PLAYED THE DOG?
CAREFUL, I MIGHT BITE!
TRY!
WATCH OUT FOR YOUR CALVES, LITTLE RASCAL!
HEE HEE
GRRR GRRR!
CATCH ME IF YOU CAN!
WOOF! WOOF!
HA HA HA
WOOF! WOOF!
POW
?
IT'S 'CAUSE THAT MUTT WAS BITING ME!

"A Big Head"

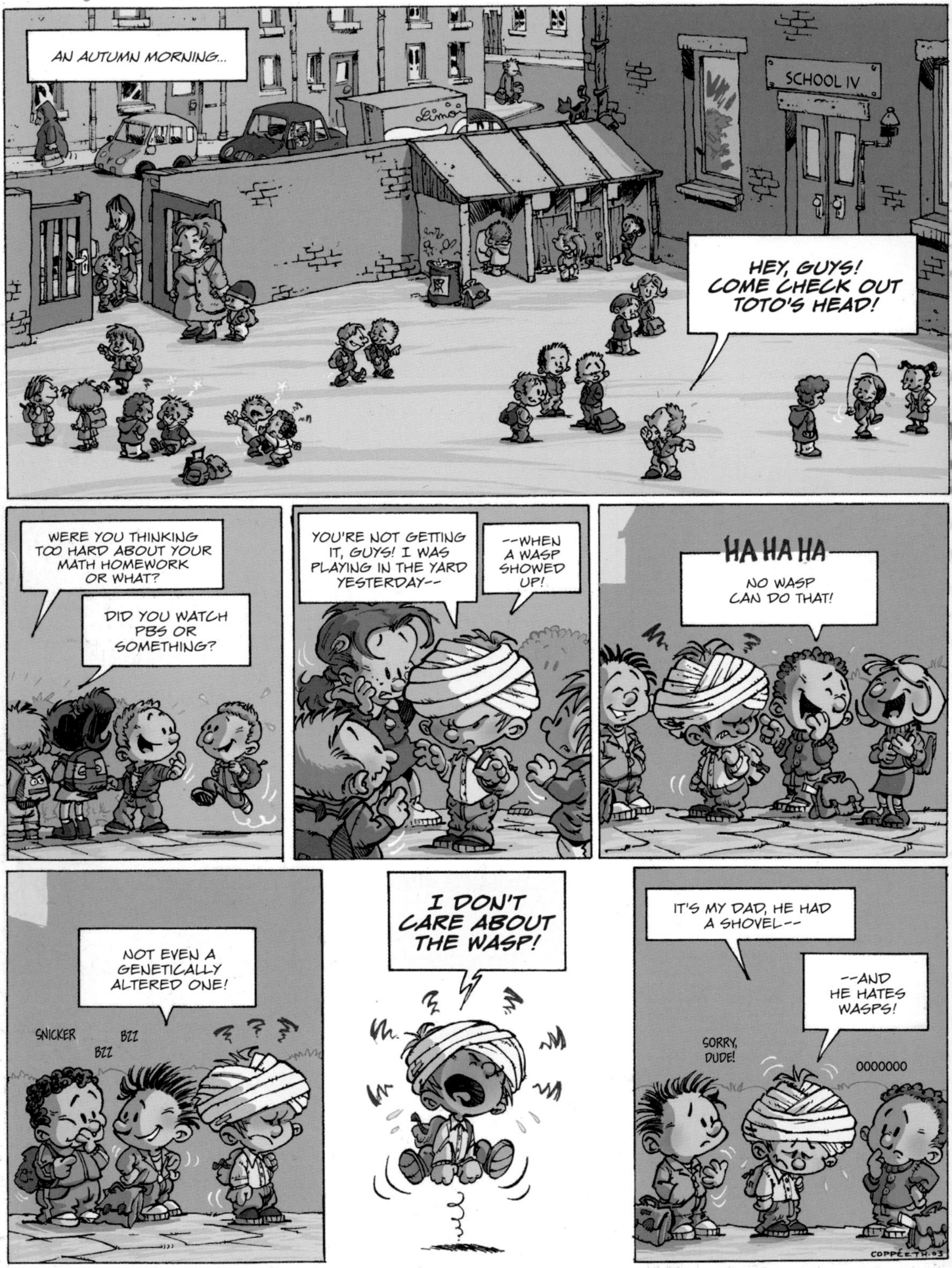

AN AUTUMN MORNING...
SCHOOL IV
HEY, GUYS! COME CHECK OUT TOTO'S HEAD!
WERE YOU THINKING TOO HARD ABOUT YOUR MATH HOMEWORK OR WHAT?
DID YOU WATCH PBS OR SOMETHING?
YOU'RE NOT GETTING IT, GUYS! I WAS PLAYING IN THE YARD YESTERDAY--
--WHEN A WASP SHOWED UP!
HA HA HA
NO WASP CAN DO THAT!
NOT EVEN A GENETICALLY ALTERED ONE!
SNICKER
BZZ
BZZ
I DON'T CARE ABOUT THE WASP!
IT'S MY DAD, HE HAD A SHOVEL--
--AND HE HATES WASPS!
SORRY, DUDE!
OOOOOOO
COPPÉE TH. 03

"The Coffin"

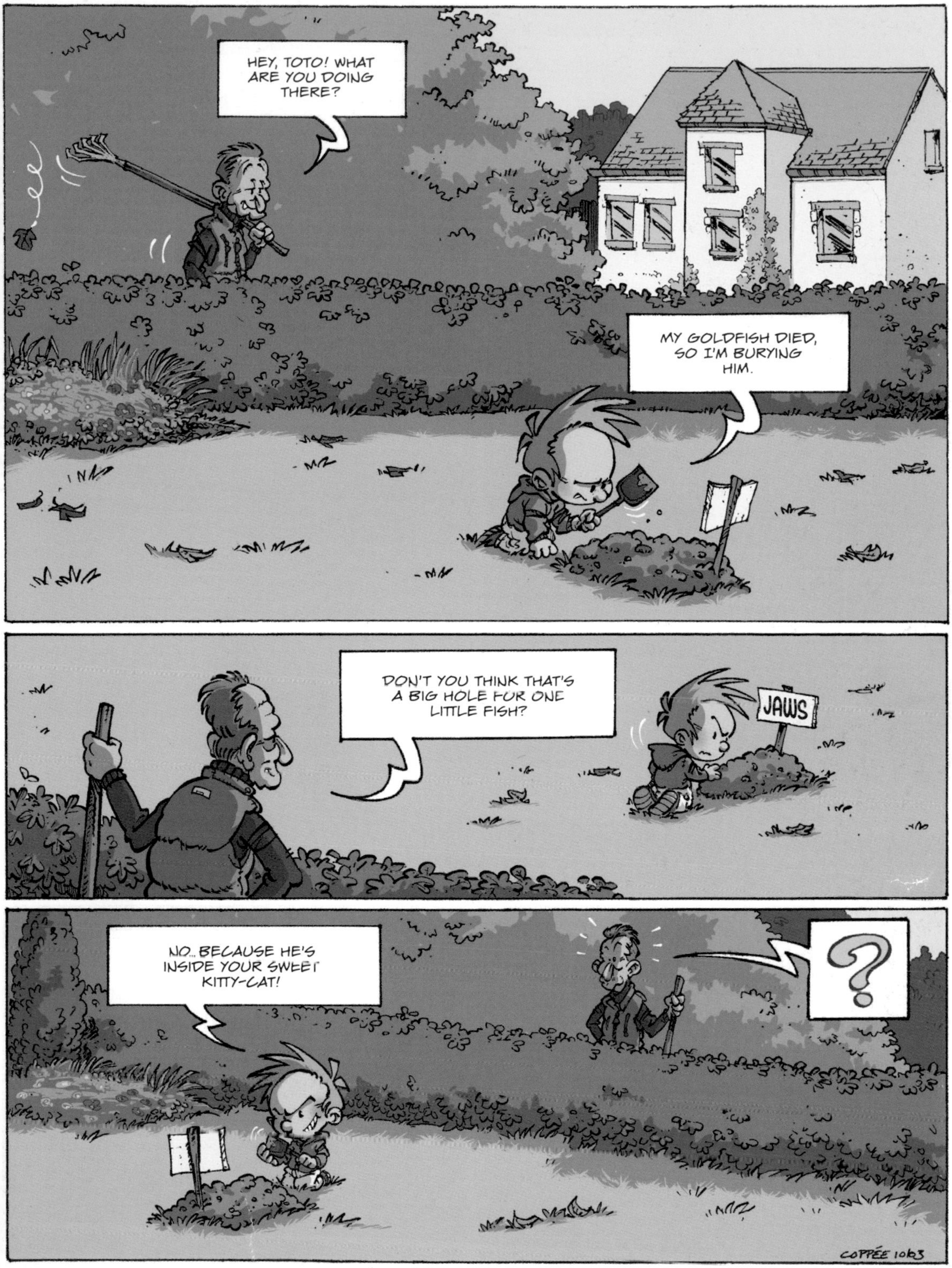
HEY, TOTO! WHAT ARE YOU DOING THERE?
MY GOLDFISH DIED, SO I'M BURYING HIM.
DON'T YOU THINK THAT'S A BIG HOLE FOR ONE LITTLE FISH?
JAWS
NO... BECAUSE HE'S INSIDE YOUR SWEET KITTY-CAT!
?
COPPÉE 10/03

"Singing the Times Table"

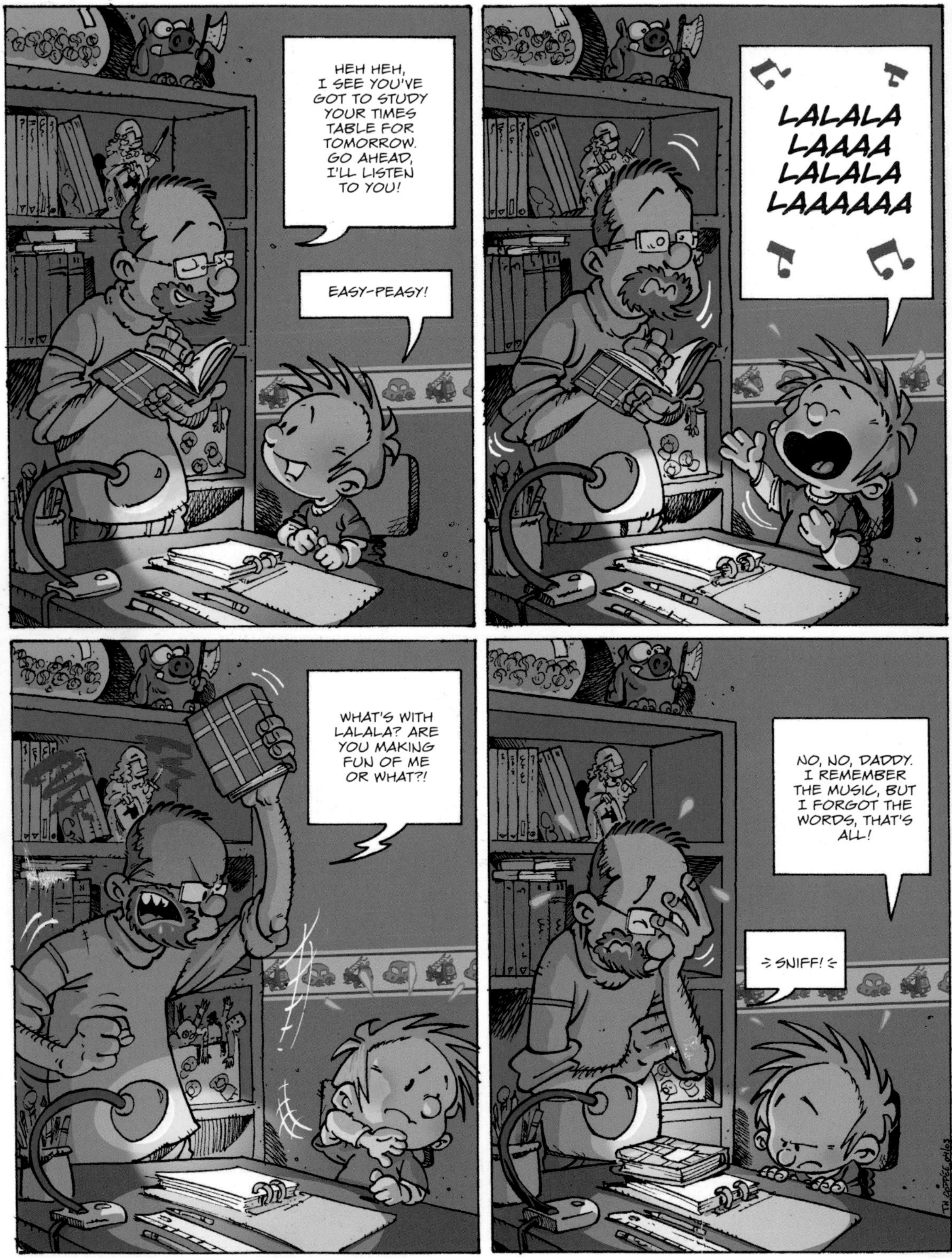
HEH HEH, I SEE YOU'VE GOT TO STUDY YOUR TIMES TABLE FOR TOMORROW. GO AHEAD, I'LL LISTEN TO YOU!
EASY-PEASY!
LALALA LAAAA LALALA LAAAAAA
WHAT'S WITH LALALA? ARE YOU MAKING FUN OF ME OR WHAT?!
NO, NO, DADDY. I REMEMBER THE MUSIC, BUT I FORGOT THE WORDS, THAT'S ALL!
SNIFF!

"After School"

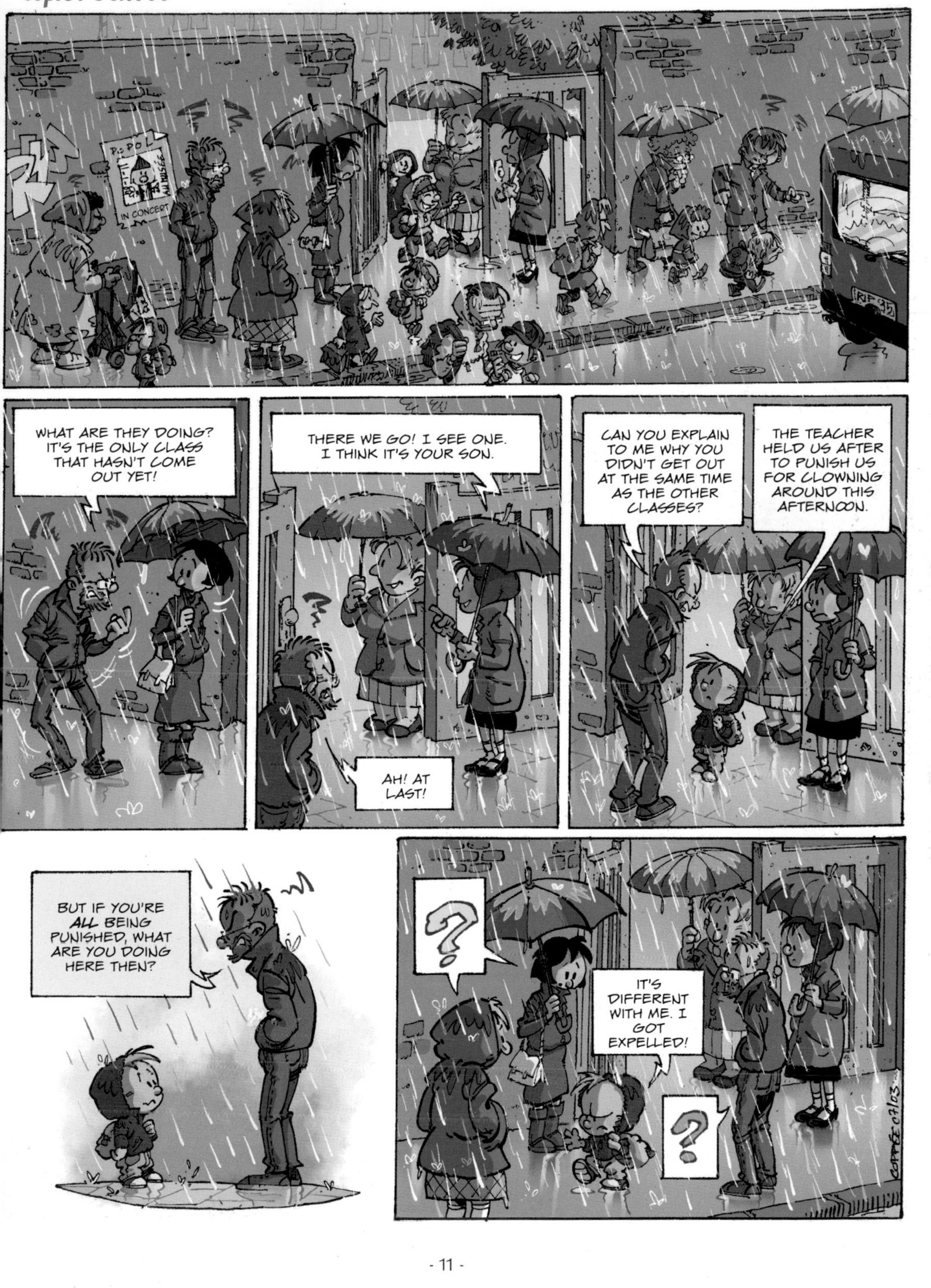
IN CONCERT
WHAT ARE THEY DOING? IT'S THE ONLY CLASS THAT HASN'T COME OUT YET!
THERE WE GO! I SEE ONE. I THINK IT'S YOUR SON.
AH! AT LAST!
CAN YOU EXPLAIN TO ME WHY YOU DIDN'T GET OUT AT THE SAME TIME AS THE OTHER CLASSES?
THE TEACHER HELD US AFTER TO PUNISH US FOR CLOWNING AROUND THIS AFTERNOON.
BUT IF YOU'RE **ALL** BEING PUNISHED, WHAT ARE YOU DOING HERE THEN?
?
IT'S DIFFERENT WITH ME. I GOT EXPELLED!
?

"Chew Your Food"

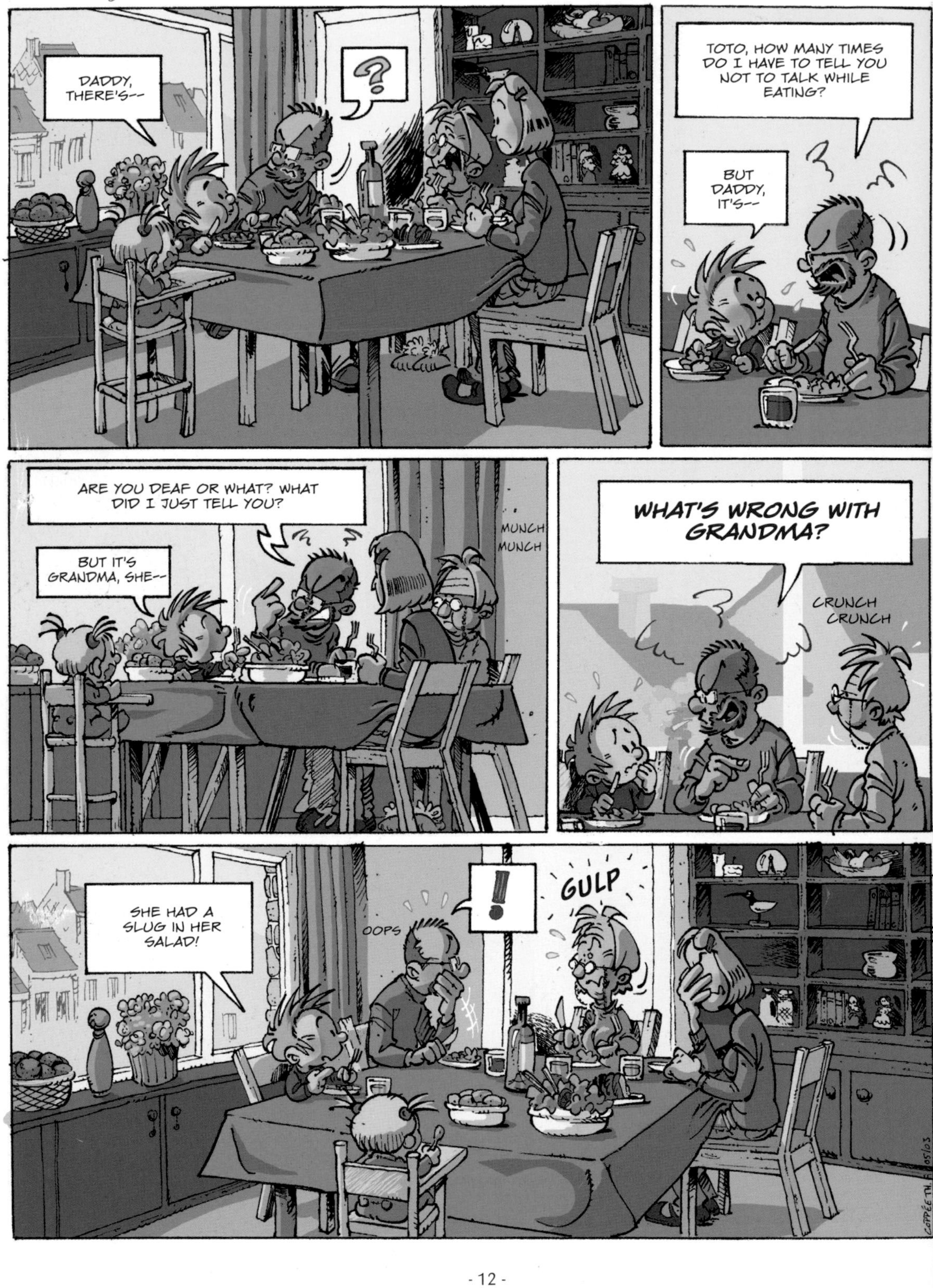
DADDY, THERE'S--
?
TOTO, HOW MANY TIMES DO I HAVE TO TELL YOU NOT TO TALK WHILE EATING?
BUT DADDY, IT'S--
ARE YOU DEAF OR WHAT? WHAT DID I JUST TELL YOU?
BUT IT'S GRANDMA, SHE--
MUNCH MUNCH
WHAT'S WRONG WITH GRANDMA?
CRUNCH CRUNCH
SHE HAD A SLUG IN HER SALAD!
OOPS
!
GULP

"The Puzzle Genius"

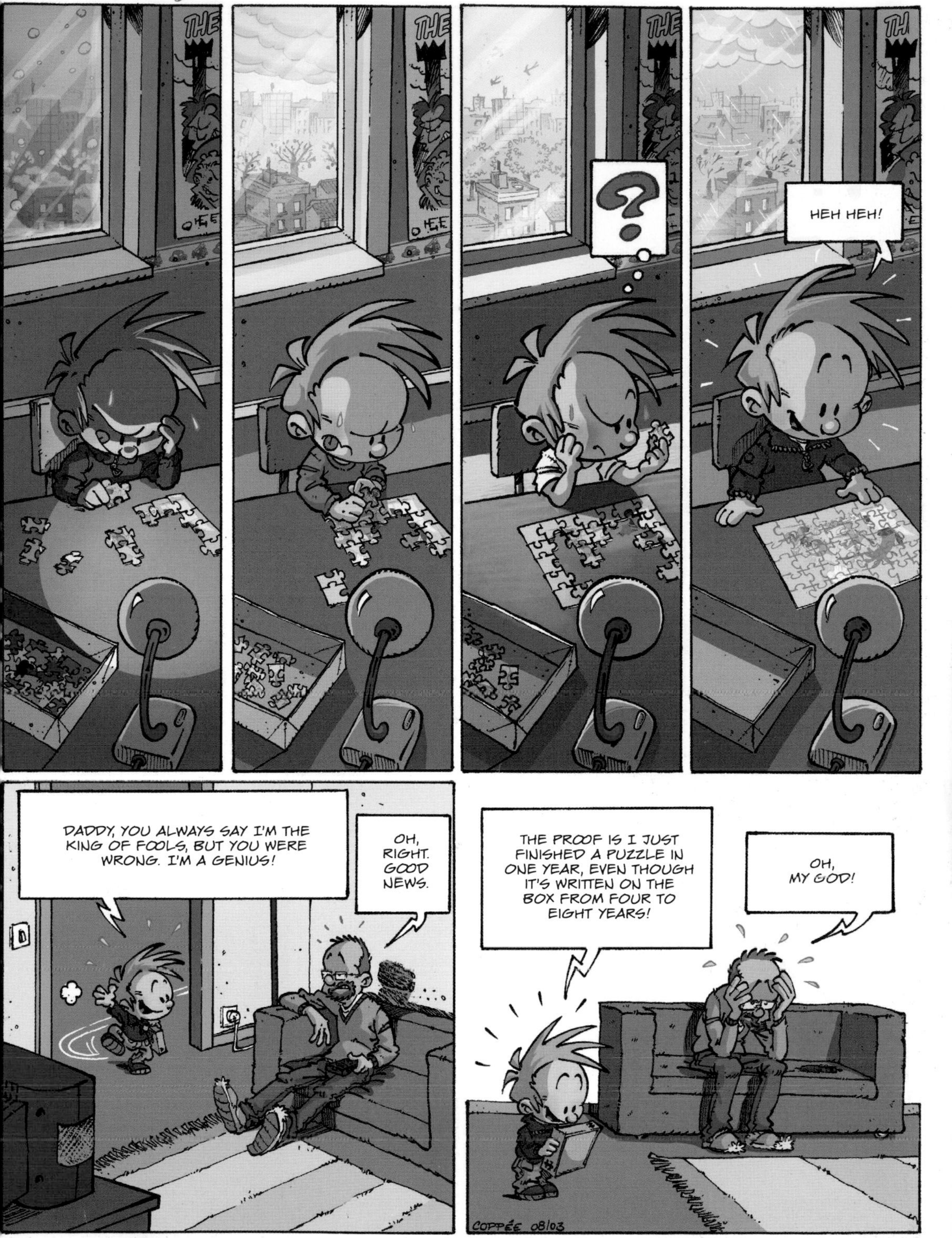
?
HEH HEH!
DADDY, YOU ALWAYS SAY I'M THE KING OF FOOLS, BUT YOU WERE WRONG. I'M A GENIUS!
OH, RIGHT. GOOD NEWS.
THE PROOF IS I JUST FINISHED A PUZZLE IN ONE YEAR, EVEN THOUGH IT'S WRITTEN ON THE BOX FROM FOUR TO EIGHT YEARS!
OH, MY GOD!
COPPÉE 08/03

"The Good Idea"

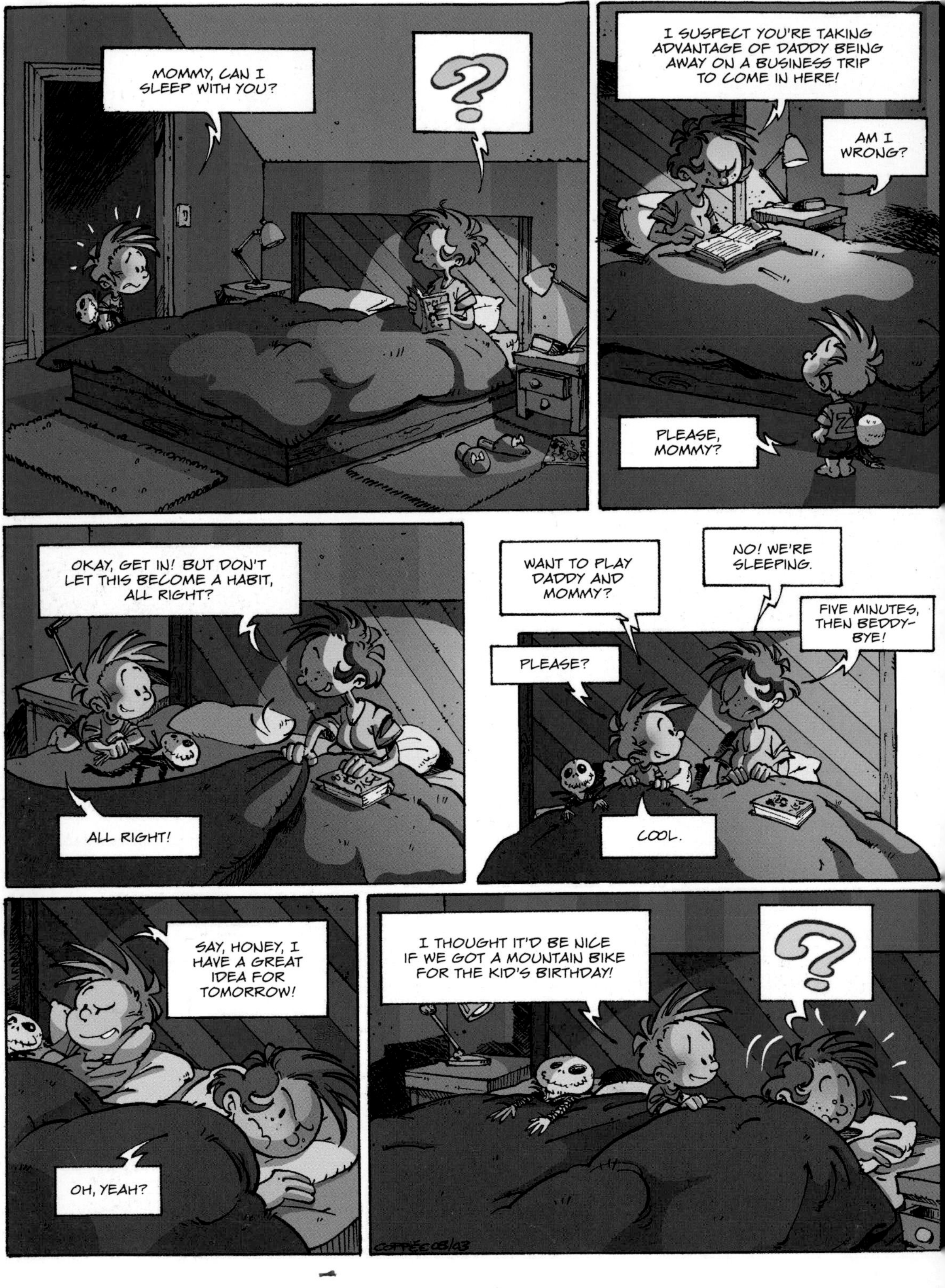

MOMMY, CAN I SLEEP WITH YOU?
?
I SUSPECT YOU'RE TAKING ADVANTAGE OF DADDY BEING AWAY ON A BUSINESS TRIP TO COME IN HERE!
AM I WRONG?
PLEASE, MOMMY?
OKAY, GET IN! BUT DON'T LET THIS BECOME A HABIT, ALL RIGHT?
ALL RIGHT!
WANT TO PLAY DADDY AND MOMMY?
NO! WE'RE SLEEPING.
FIVE MINUTES, THEN BEDDY-BYE!
PLEASE?
COOL.
SAY, HONEY, I HAVE A GREAT IDEA FOR TOMORROW!
OH, YEAH?
I THOUGHT IT'D BE NICE IF WE GOT A MOUNTAIN BIKE FOR THE KID'S BIRTHDAY!
?
COPPÉE 08/03

"Suggested Detergent"

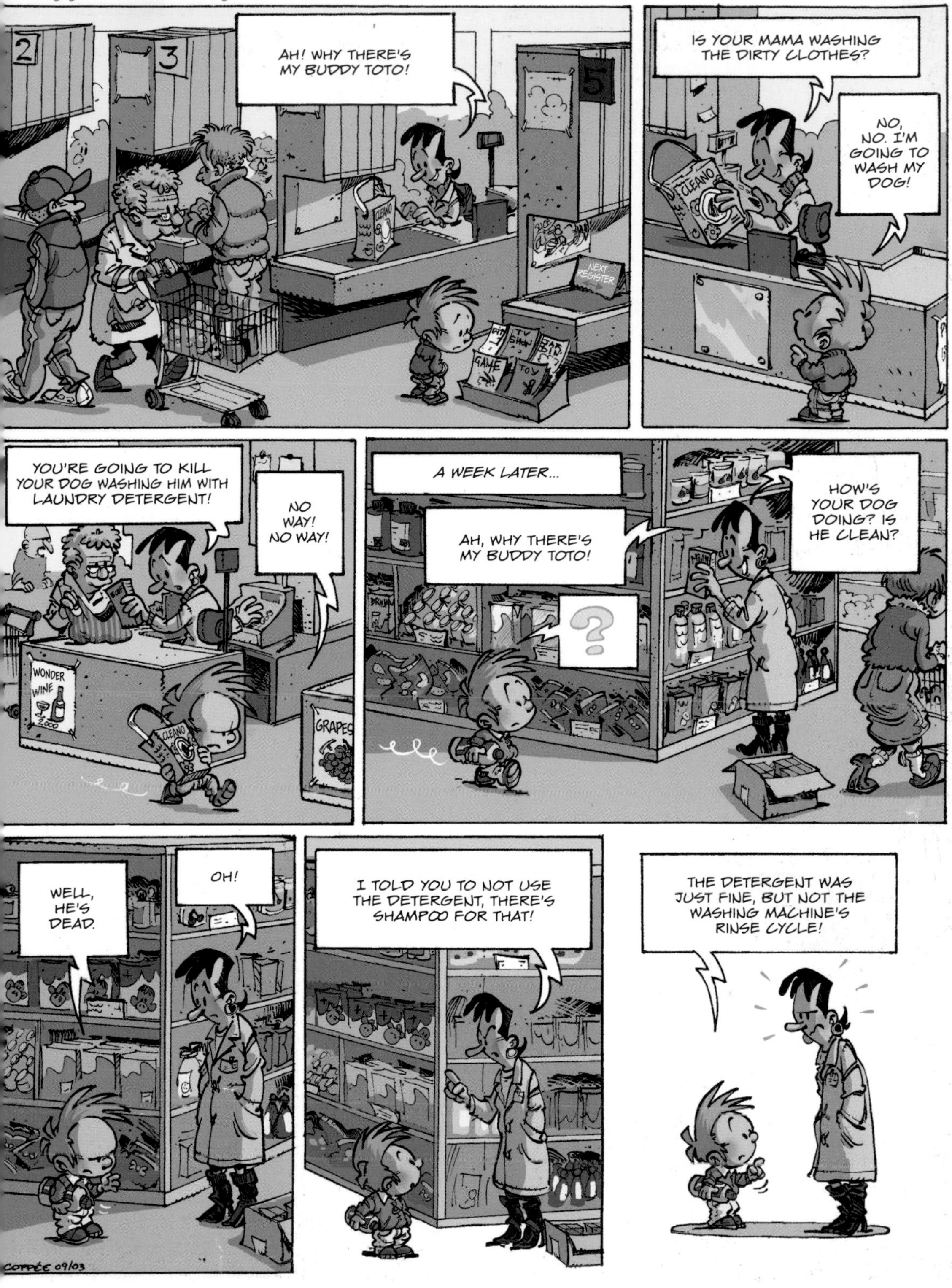

AH! WHY THERE'S MY BUDDY TOTO!
IS YOUR MAMA WASHING THE DIRTY CLOTHES?
NO, NO. I'M GOING TO WASH MY DOG!
YOU'RE GOING TO KILL YOUR DOG WASHING HIM WITH LAUNDRY DETERGENT!
NO WAY! NO WAY!
A WEEK LATER...
AH, WHY THERE'S MY BUDDY TOTO!
HOW'S YOUR DOG DOING? IS HE CLEAN?
?
WELL, HE'S DEAD.
OH!
I TOLD YOU TO NOT USE THE DETERGENT, THERE'S SHAMPOO FOR THAT!
THE DETERGENT WAS JUST FINE, BUT NOT THE WASHING MACHINE'S RINSE CYCLE!

"The Martyr"

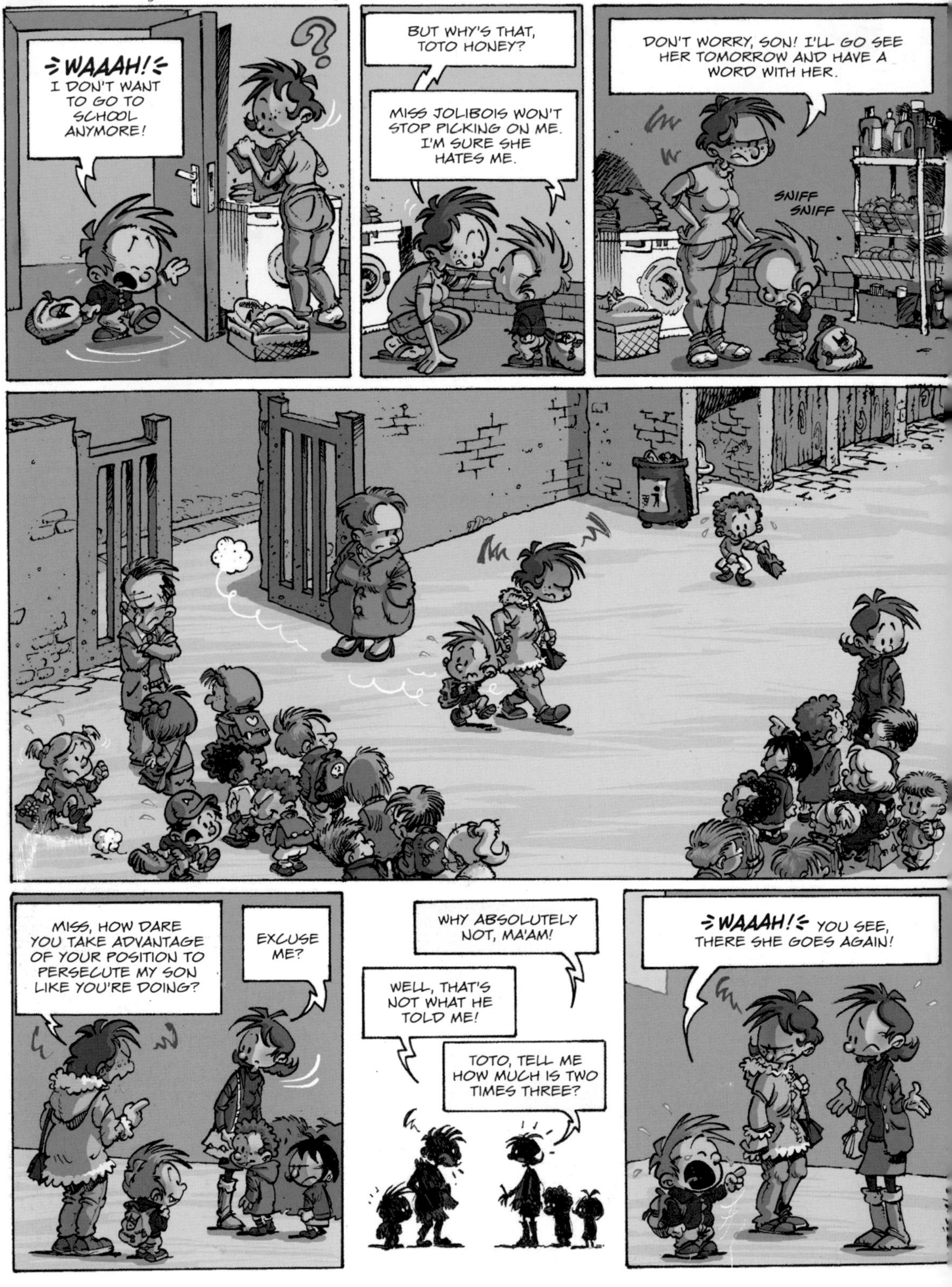
WAAAH! I DON'T WANT TO GO TO SCHOOL ANYMORE!
BUT WHY'S THAT, TOTO HONEY?
MISS JOLIBOIS WON'T STOP PICKING ON ME. I'M SURE SHE HATES ME.
DON'T WORRY, SON! I'LL GO SEE HER TOMORROW AND HAVE A WORD WITH HER.
SNIFF SNIFF
MISS, HOW DARE YOU TAKE ADVANTAGE OF YOUR POSITION TO PERSECUTE MY SON LIKE YOU'RE DOING?
EXCUSE ME?
WHY ABSOLUTELY NOT, MA'AM!
WELL, THAT'S NOT WHAT HE TOLD ME!
TOTO, TELL ME HOW MUCH IS TWO TIMES THREE?
WAAAH! YOU SEE, THERE SHE GOES AGAIN!

"The Changing Room"

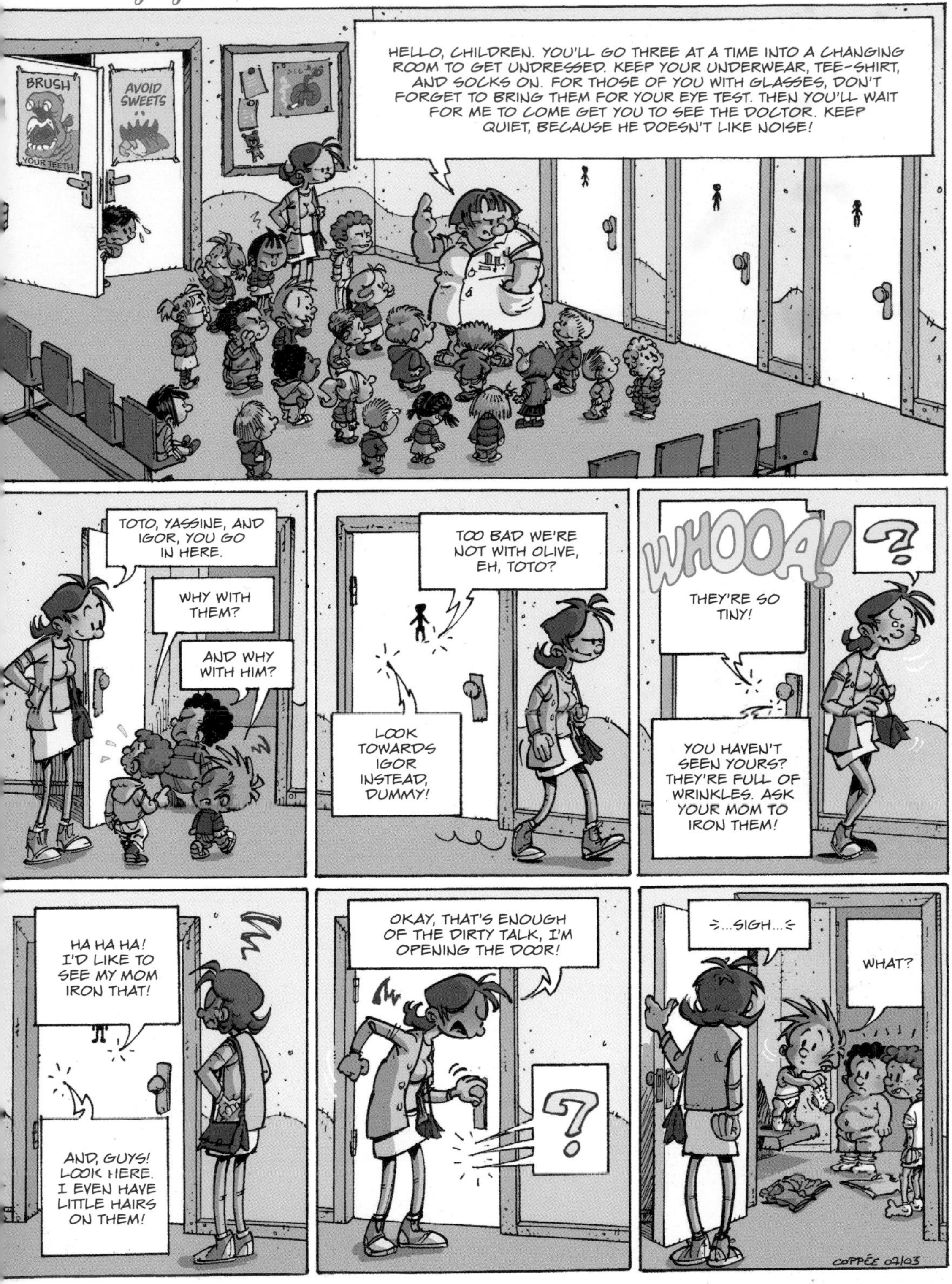

BRUSH
YOUR TEETH
AVOID SWEETS
HELLO, CHILDREN. YOU'LL GO THREE AT A TIME INTO A CHANGING ROOM TO GET UNDRESSED. KEEP YOUR UNDERWEAR, TEE-SHIRT, AND SOCKS ON. FOR THOSE OF YOU WITH GLASSES, DON'T FORGET TO BRING THEM FOR YOUR EYE TEST. THEN YOU'LL WAIT FOR ME TO COME GET YOU TO SEE THE DOCTOR. KEEP QUIET, BECAUSE HE DOESN'T LIKE NOISE!
TOTO, YASSINE, AND IGOR, YOU GO IN HERE.
WHY WITH THEM?
AND WHY WITH HIM?
TOO BAD WE'RE NOT WITH OLIVE, EH, TOTO?
LOOK TOWARDS IGOR INSTEAD, DUMMY!
WHOOA!
?
THEY'RE SO TINY!
YOU HAVEN'T SEEN YOURS? THEY'RE FULL OF WRINKLES. ASK YOUR MOM TO IRON THEM!
HA HA HA! I'D LIKE TO SEE MY MOM IRON THAT!
AND, GUYS! LOOK HERE. I EVEN HAVE LITTLE HAIRS ON THEM!
OKAY, THAT'S ENOUGH OF THE DIRTY TALK, I'M OPENING THE DOOR!
?
...SIGH...
WHAT?
COPPÉE 07/03

"A Logical Method"

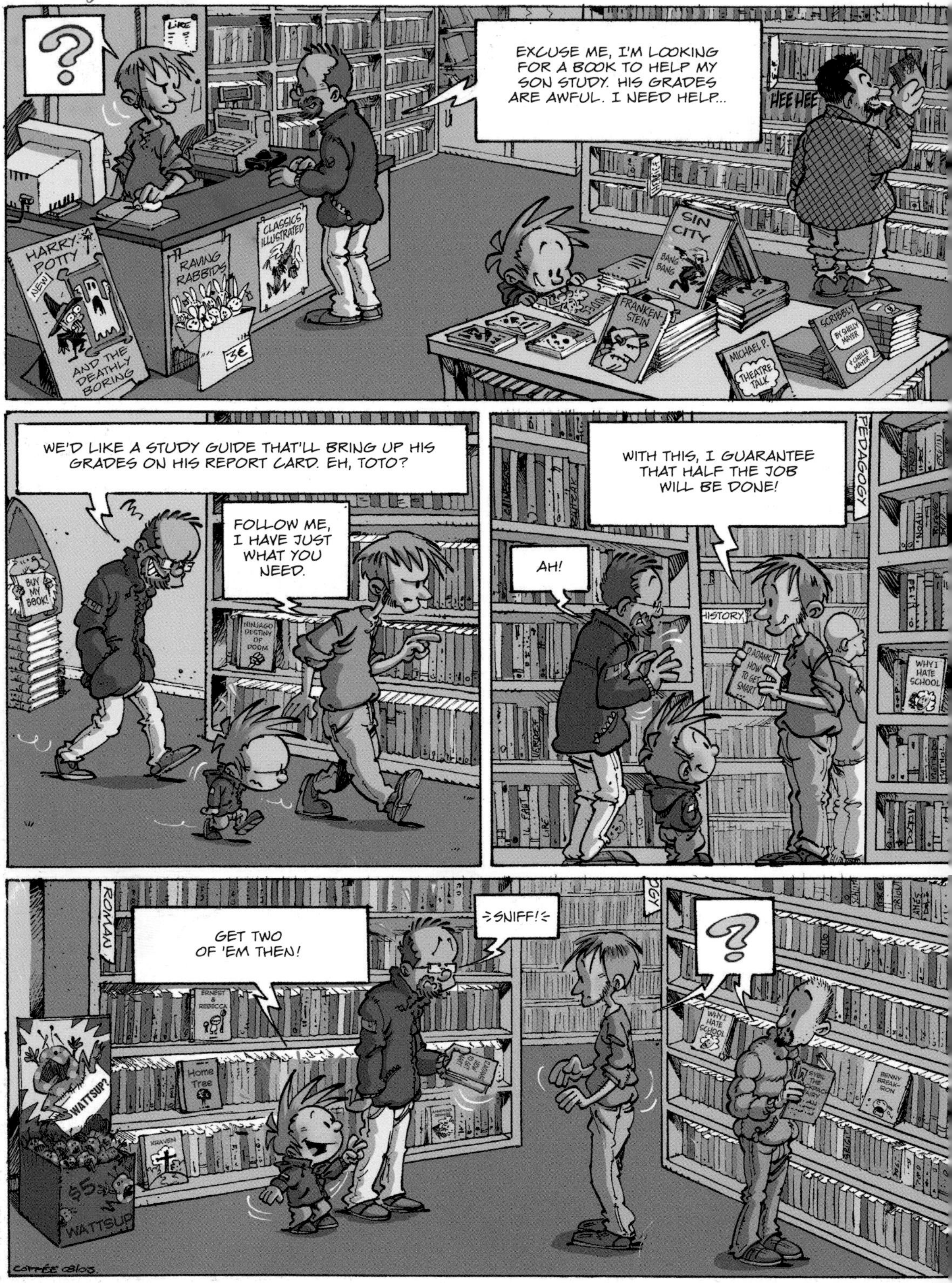
?
EXCUSE ME, I'M LOOKING FOR A BOOK TO HELP MY SON STUDY. HIS GRADES ARE AWFUL. I NEED HELP...
HEE HEE
HARRY POTTY AND THE DEATHLY BORING
RAVING RABBIDS
CLASSICS ILLUSTRATED
SIN CITY
FRANKENSTEIN
SCRIBBLY
MICHAEL P. THEATRE TALK
WE'D LIKE A STUDY GUIDE THAT'LL BRING UP HIS GRADES ON HIS REPORT CARD. EH, TOTO?
FOLLOW ME, I HAVE JUST WHAT YOU NEED.
BUY MY BOOK!
NINJAGO DESTINY OF DOOM
WITH THIS, I GUARANTEE THAT HALF THE JOB WILL BE DONE!
AH!
PEDAGOGY
HISTORY
D. ADAMS HOW TO GET SMART
WHY I HATE SCHOOL
GET TWO OF 'EM THEN!
SNIFF!
?
ROMAN
ERNEST & REBECCA
Home Tree
KRAVEN
WATTSUP?
$5
WHY I HATE SCHOOL
BENNY BREAKIRON

"Seeing Red"

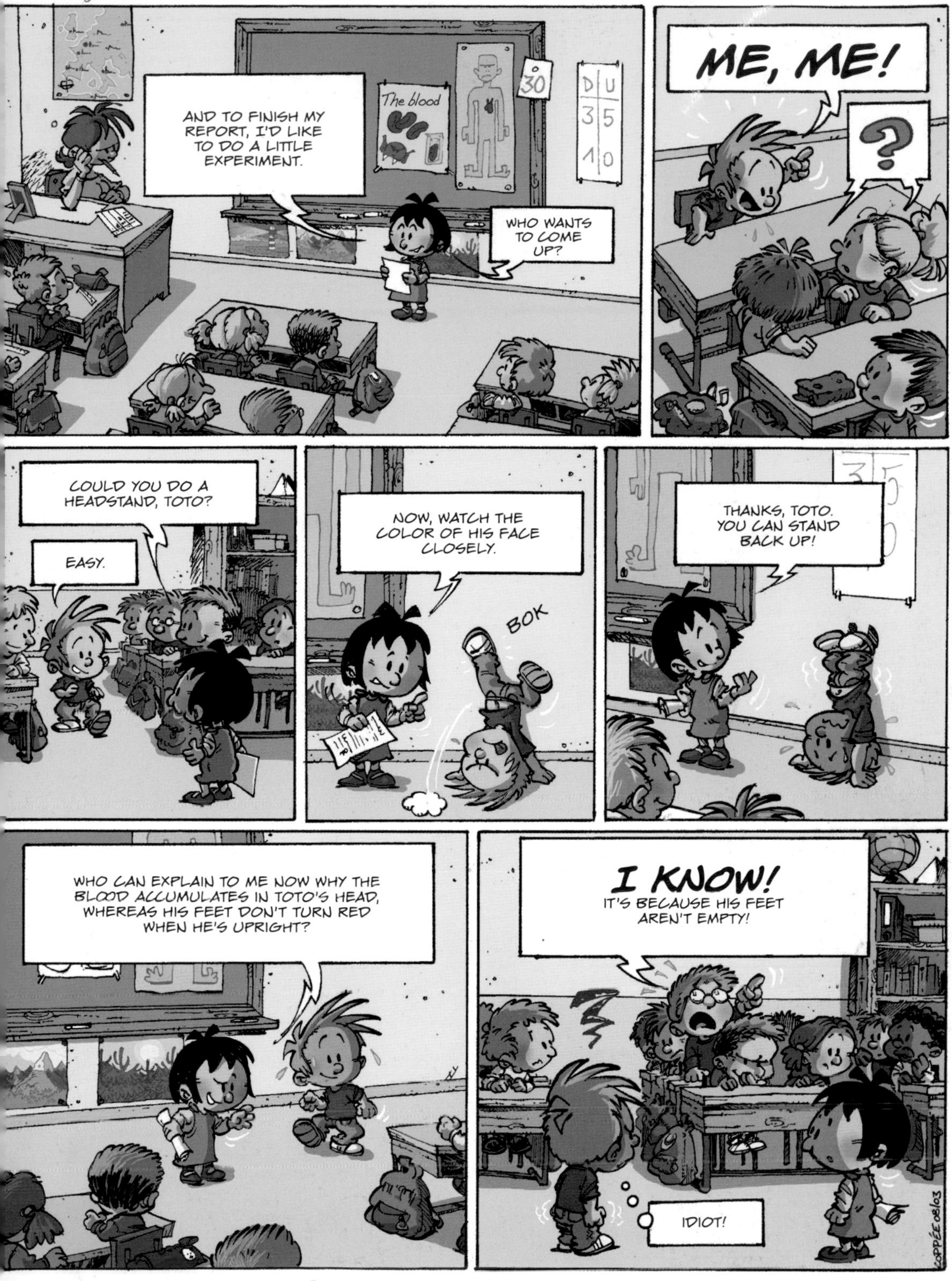

AND TO FINISH MY REPORT, I'D LIKE TO DO A LITTLE EXPERIMENT.
WHO WANTS TO COME UP?
The blood
ME, ME!
?
COULD YOU DO A HEADSTAND, TOTO?
EASY.
NOW, WATCH THE COLOR OF HIS FACE CLOSELY.
BOK
THANKS, TOTO. YOU CAN STAND BACK UP!
WHO CAN EXPLAIN TO ME NOW WHY THE BLOOD ACCUMULATES IN TOTO'S HEAD, WHEREAS HIS FEET DON'T TURN RED WHEN HE'S UPRIGHT?
I KNOW!
IT'S BECAUSE HIS FEET AREN'T EMPTY!
IDIOT!
COPPÉE 08/03

"Find the Mistake"

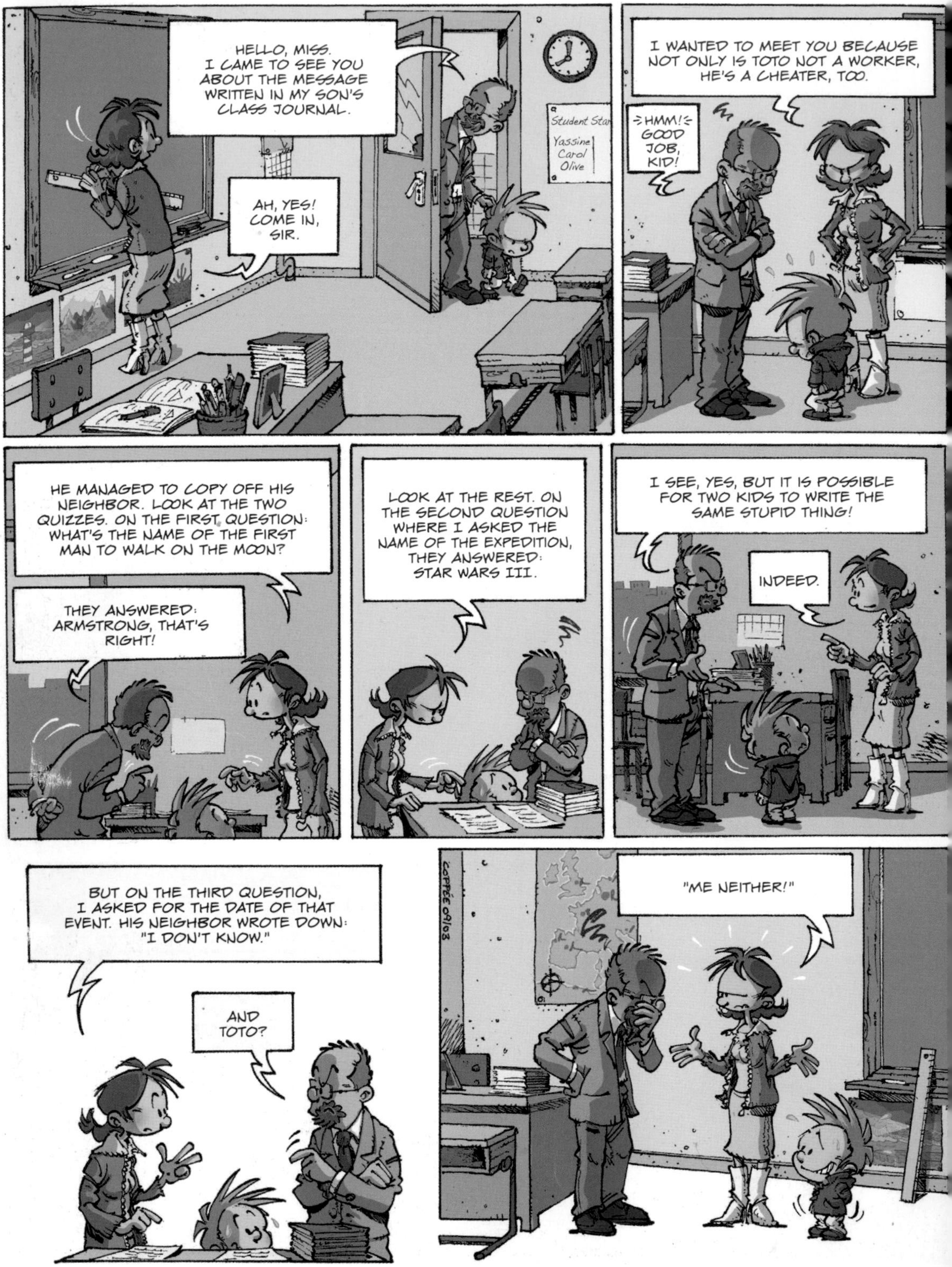

HELLO, MISS. I CAME TO SEE YOU ABOUT THE MESSAGE WRITTEN IN MY SON'S CLASS JOURNAL.
AH, YES! COME IN, SIR.
Student Star
Yassine
Carol
Olive
I WANTED TO MEET YOU BECAUSE NOT ONLY IS TOTO NOT A WORKER, HE'S A CHEATER, TOO.
HMM! GOOD JOB, KID!
HE MANAGED TO COPY OFF HIS NEIGHBOR. LOOK AT THE TWO QUIZZES. ON THE FIRST QUESTION: WHAT'S THE NAME OF THE FIRST MAN TO WALK ON THE MOON?
THEY ANSWERED: ARMSTRONG, THAT'S RIGHT!
LOOK AT THE REST. ON THE SECOND QUESTION WHERE I ASKED THE NAME OF THE EXPEDITION, THEY ANSWERED: STAR WARS III.
I SEE, YES, BUT IT IS POSSIBLE FOR TWO KIDS TO WRITE THE SAME STUPID THING!
INDEED.
BUT ON THE THIRD QUESTION, I ASKED FOR THE DATE OF THAT EVENT. HIS NEIGHBOR WROTE DOWN: "I DON'T KNOW."
AND TOTO?
COPPÉE 09/03
"ME NEITHER!"

"The Hypochondriac"

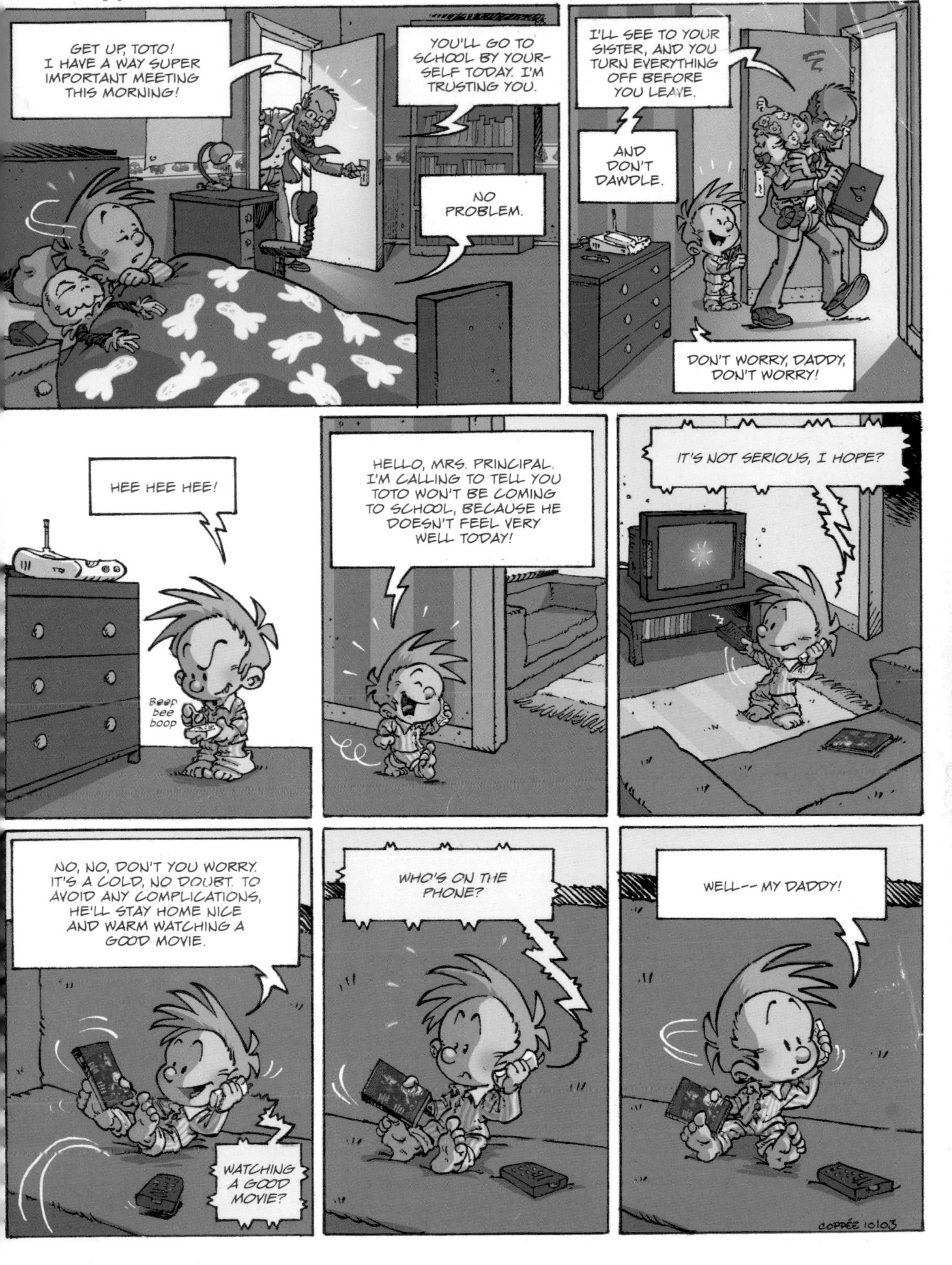
GET UP, TOTO! I HAVE A WAY SUPER IMPORTANT MEETING THIS MORNING!
YOU'LL GO TO SCHOOL BY YOURSELF TODAY. I'M TRUSTING YOU.
NO PROBLEM.
I'LL SEE TO YOUR SISTER, AND YOU TURN EVERYTHING OFF BEFORE YOU LEAVE.
AND DON'T DAWDLE.
DON'T WORRY, DADDY, DON'T WORRY!
HEE HEE HEE!
Beep bee boop
HELLO, MRS. PRINCIPAL. I'M CALLING TO TELL YOU TOTO WON'T BE COMING TO SCHOOL, BECAUSE HE DOESN'T FEEL VERY WELL TODAY!
IT'S NOT SERIOUS, I HOPE?
NO, NO, DON'T YOU WORRY. IT'S A COLD, NO DOUBT. TO AVOID ANY COMPLICATIONS, HE'LL STAY HOME NICE AND WARM WATCHING A GOOD MOVIE.
WATCHING A GOOD MOVIE?
WHO'S ON THE PHONE?
WELL-- MY DADDY!
COPPÉE 10.03

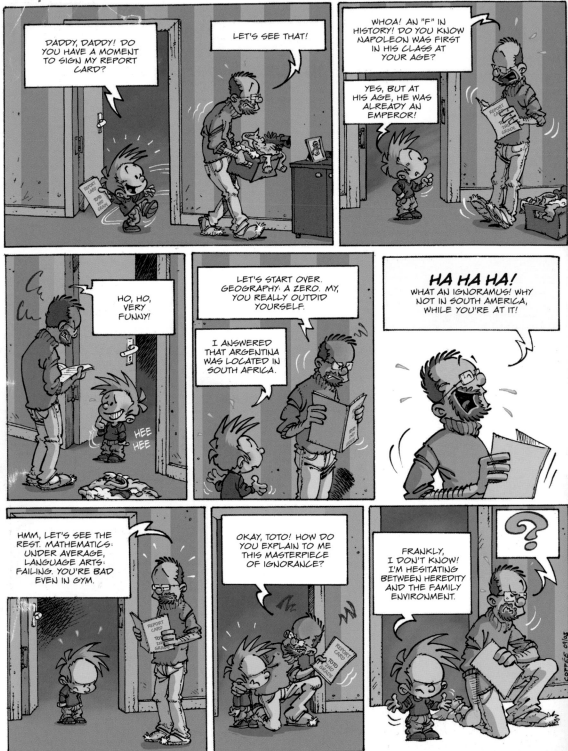

"Photo Souvenir"

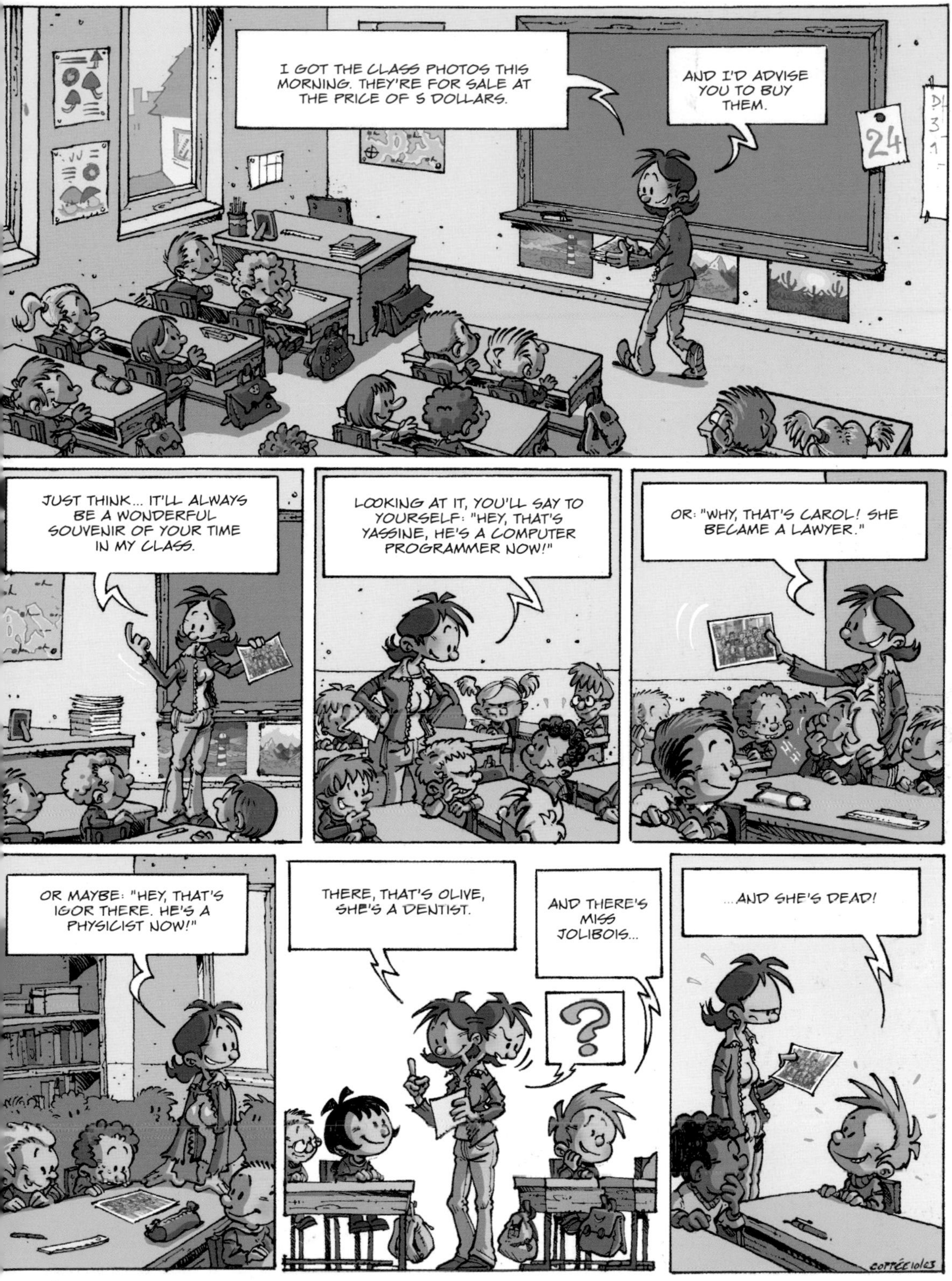
I GOT THE CLASS PHOTOS THIS MORNING. THEY'RE FOR SALE AT THE PRICE OF 5 DOLLARS.
AND I'D ADVISE YOU TO BUY THEM.
24
JUST THINK... IT'LL ALWAYS BE A WONDERFUL SOUVENIR OF YOUR TIME IN MY CLASS.
LOOKING AT IT, YOU'LL SAY TO YOURSELF: "HEY, THAT'S YASSINE, HE'S A COMPUTER PROGRAMMER NOW!"
OR: "WHY, THAT'S CAROL! SHE BECAME A LAWYER."
OR MAYBE: "HEY, THAT'S IGOR THERE. HE'S A PHYSICIST NOW!"
THERE, THAT'S OLIVE, SHE'S A DENTIST.
AND THERE'S MISS JOLIBOIS...
?
...AND SHE'S DEAD!

"Better Safe than Sorry"

"Shut Up"

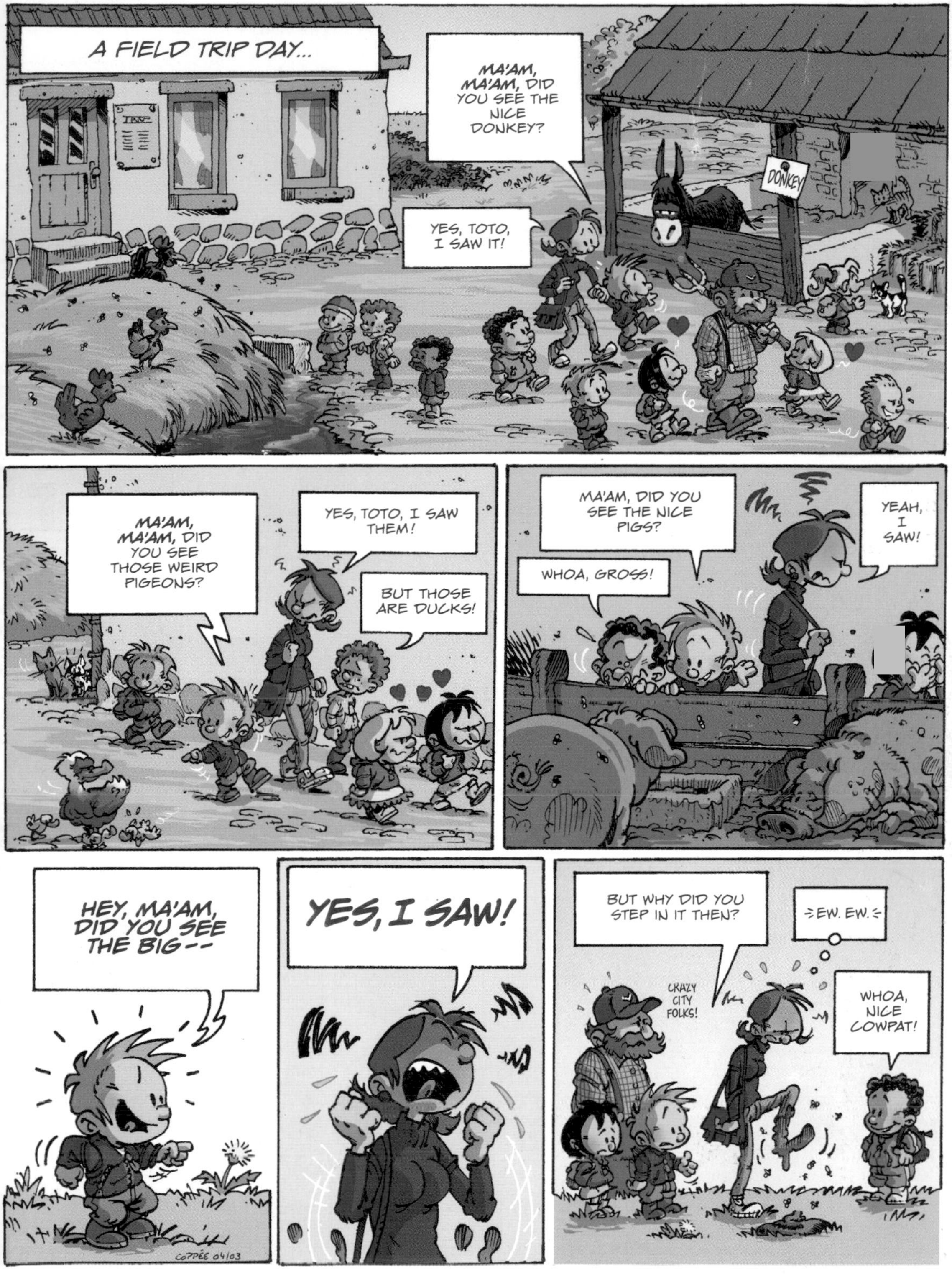
A FIELD TRIP DAY...
MA'AM, MA'AM, DID YOU SEE THE NICE DONKEY?
DONKEY
YES, TOTO, I SAW IT!
MA'AM, MA'AM, DID YOU SEE THOSE WEIRD PIGEONS?
YES, TOTO, I SAW THEM!
BUT THOSE ARE DUCKS!
MA'AM, DID YOU SEE THE NICE PIGS?
YEAH, I SAW!
WHOA, GROSS!
HEY, MA'AM, DID YOU SEE THE BIG--
COPPÉE 04/03
YES, I SAW!
BUT WHY DID YOU STEP IN IT THEN?
EW. EW.
CRAZY CITY FOLKS!
WHOA, NICE COWPAT!

"The Acrobat"

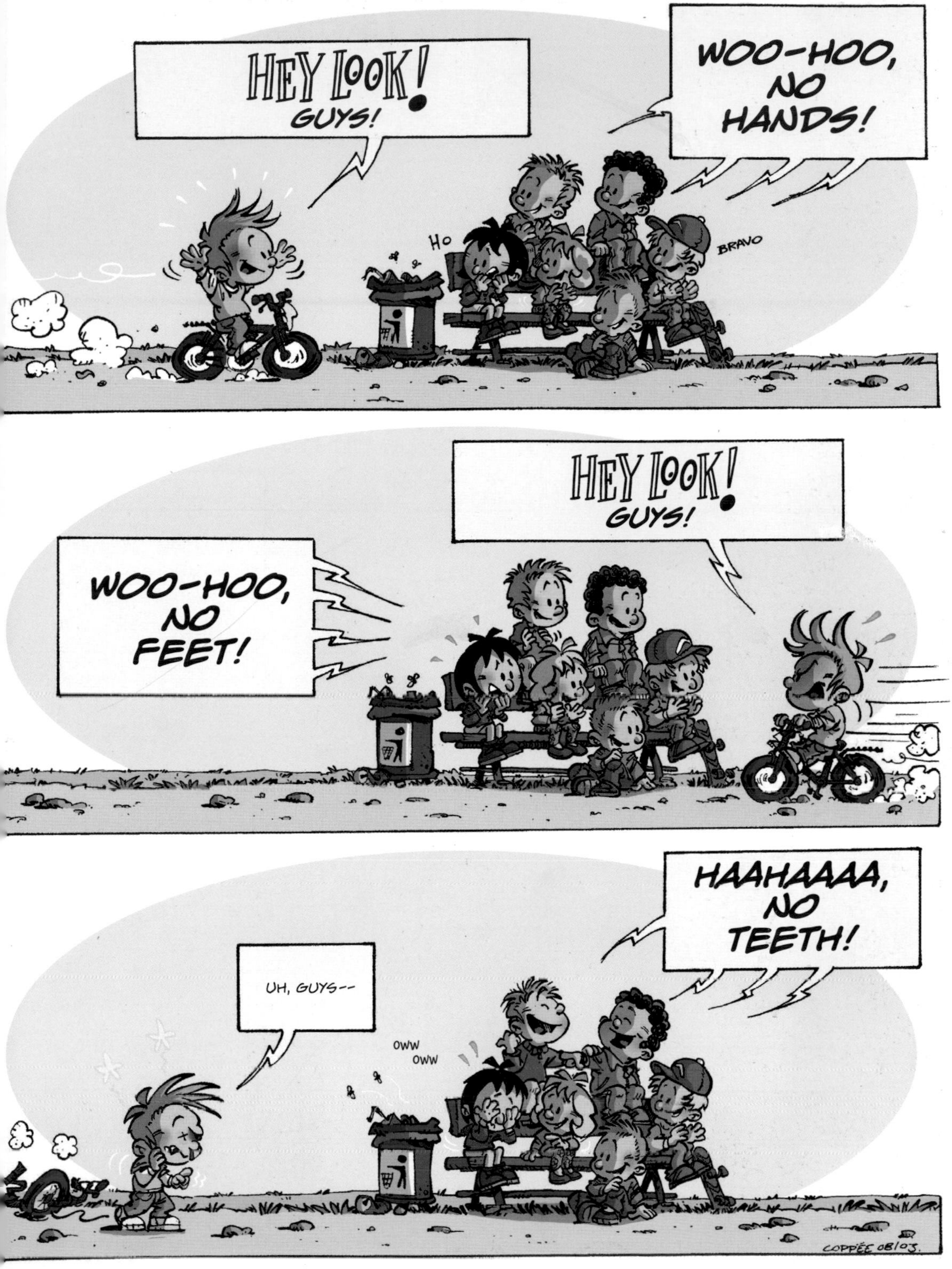
HEY LOOK! GUYS!
WOO-HOO, NO HANDS!
HO
BRAVO
HEY LOOK! GUYS!
WOO-HOO, NO FEET!
HAAHAAAA, NO TEETH!
UH, GUYS--
OWW OWW
COPPÉE 08/03.

"Red Currants"

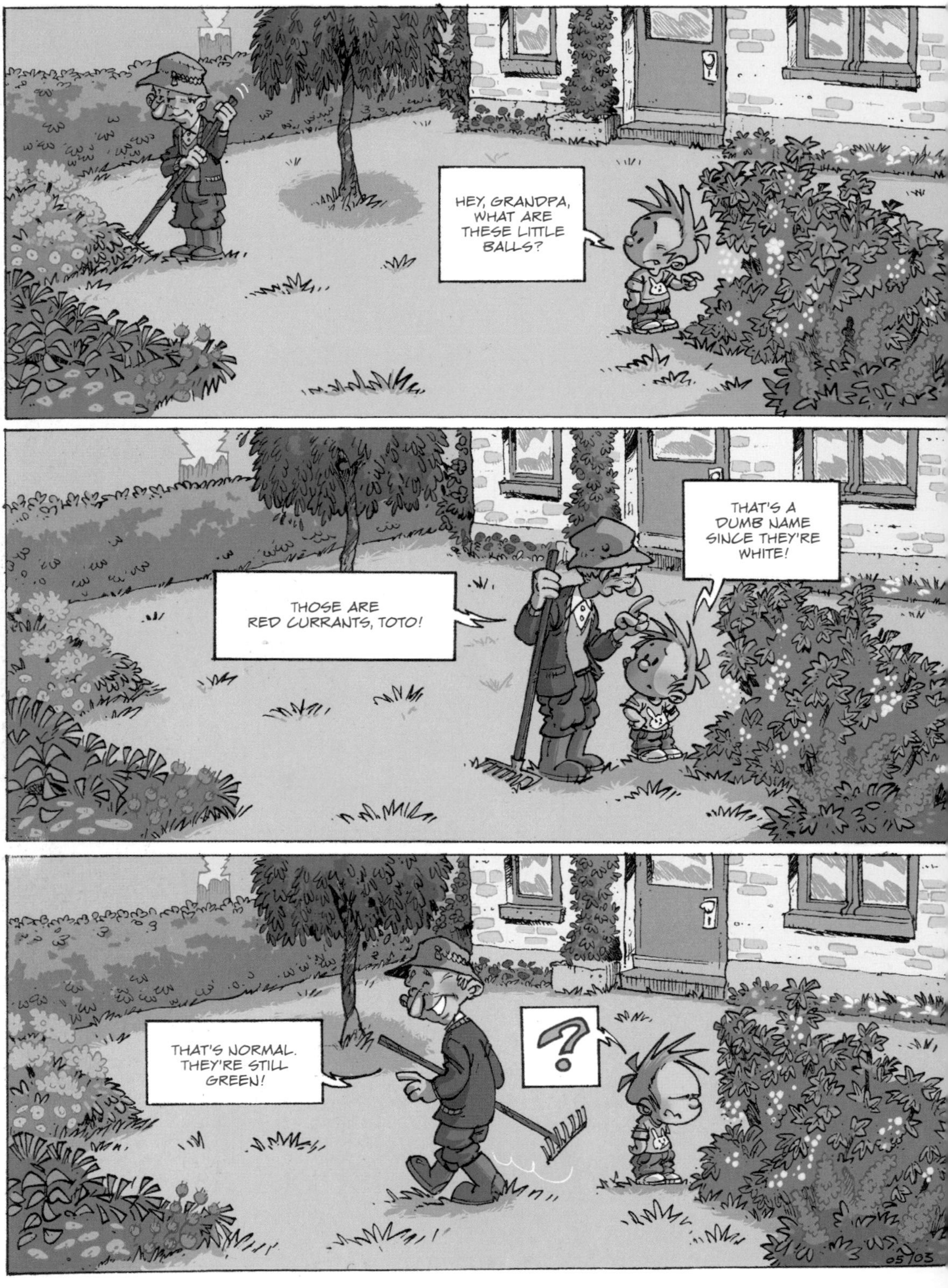
HEY, GRANDPA, WHAT ARE THESE LITTLE BALLS?
THOSE ARE RED CURRANTS, TOTO!
THAT'S A DUMB NAME SINCE THEY'RE WHITE!
THAT'S NORMAL. THEY'RE STILL GREEN!
?
05/03

"End-of-the-Year Gift"

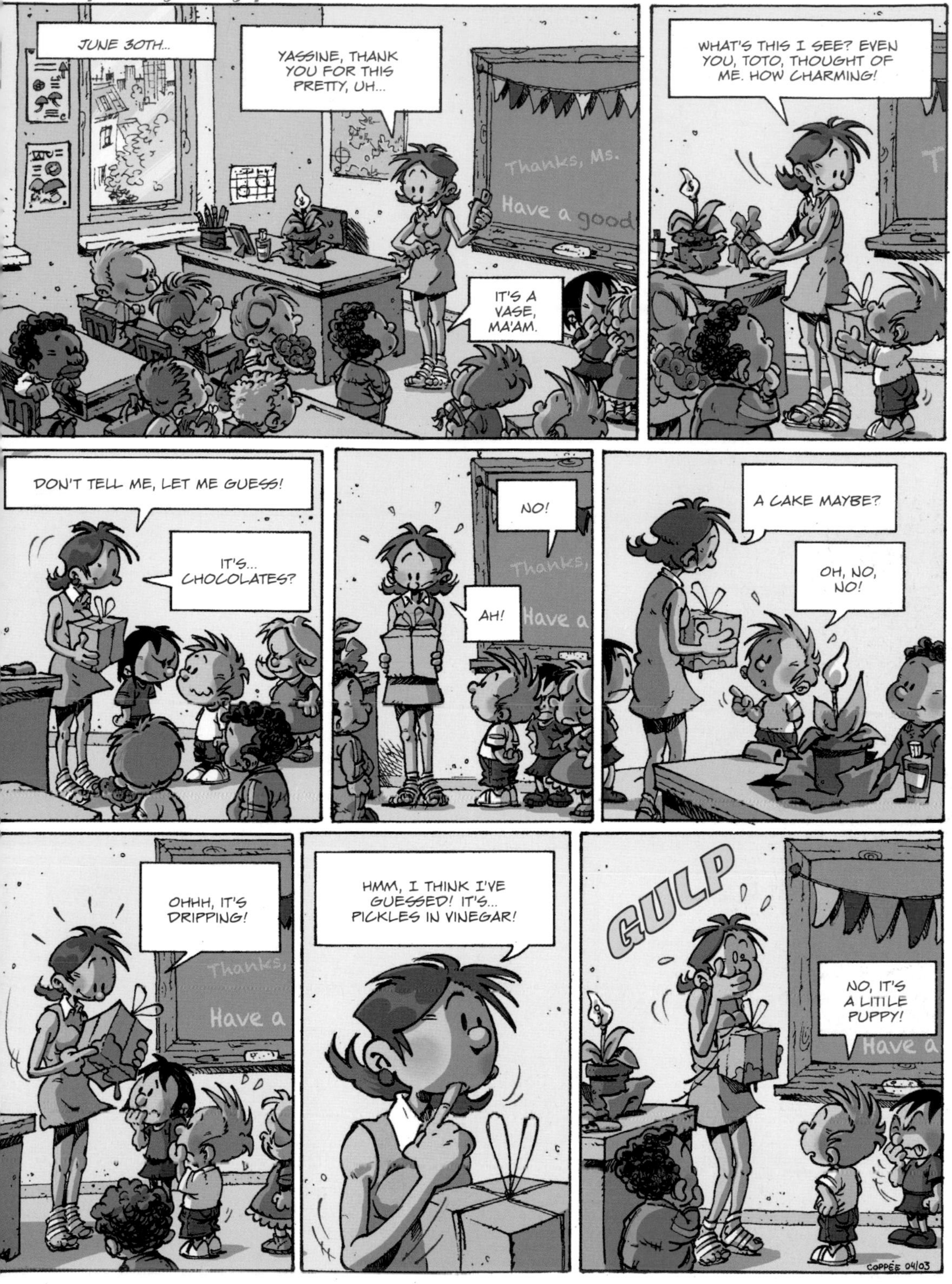

JUNE 30TH...
YASSINE, THANK YOU FOR THIS PRETTY, UH...
IT'S A VASE, MA'AM.
Thanks, Ms.
Have a good
WHAT'S THIS I SEE? EVEN YOU, TOTO, THOUGHT OF ME. HOW CHARMING!
DON'T TELL ME, LET ME GUESS!
IT'S... CHOCOLATES?
NO!
AH!
A CAKE MAYBE?
OH, NO, NO!
OHHH, IT'S DRIPPING!
HMM, I THINK I'VE GUESSED! IT'S... PICKLES IN VINEGAR!
GULP
NO, IT'S A LITTLE PUPPY!
COPPÉE 04/03

"Questions for a Champion-- The Finale"

"There Once was a Little Ship"

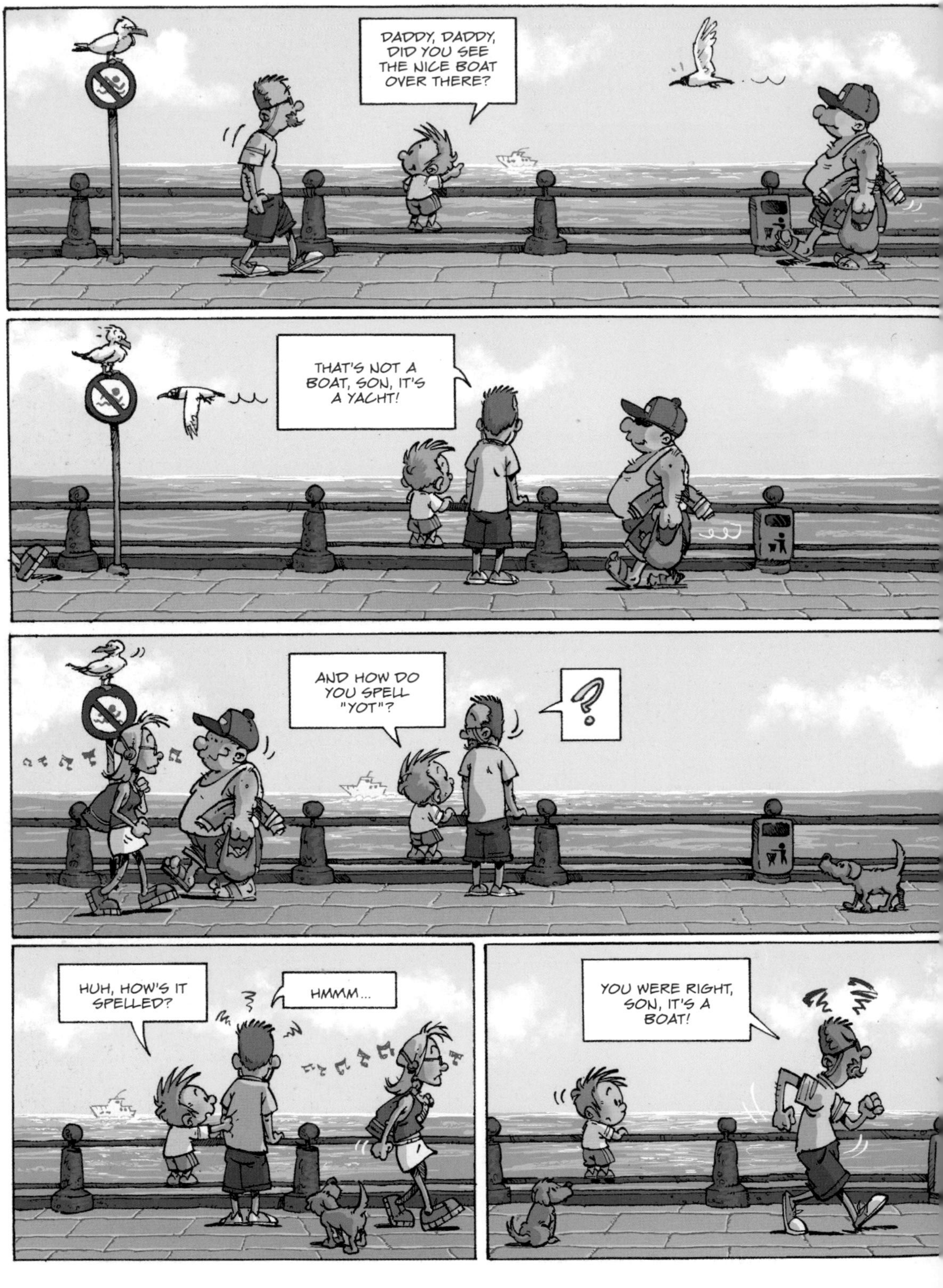
DADDY, DADDY, DID YOU SEE THE NICE BOAT OVER THERE?
THAT'S NOT A BOAT, SON, IT'S A YACHT!
AND HOW DO YOU SPELL "YOT"?
?
HUH, HOW'S IT SPELLED?
HMMM...
YOU WERE RIGHT, SON, IT'S A BOAT!

"Just Desserts"

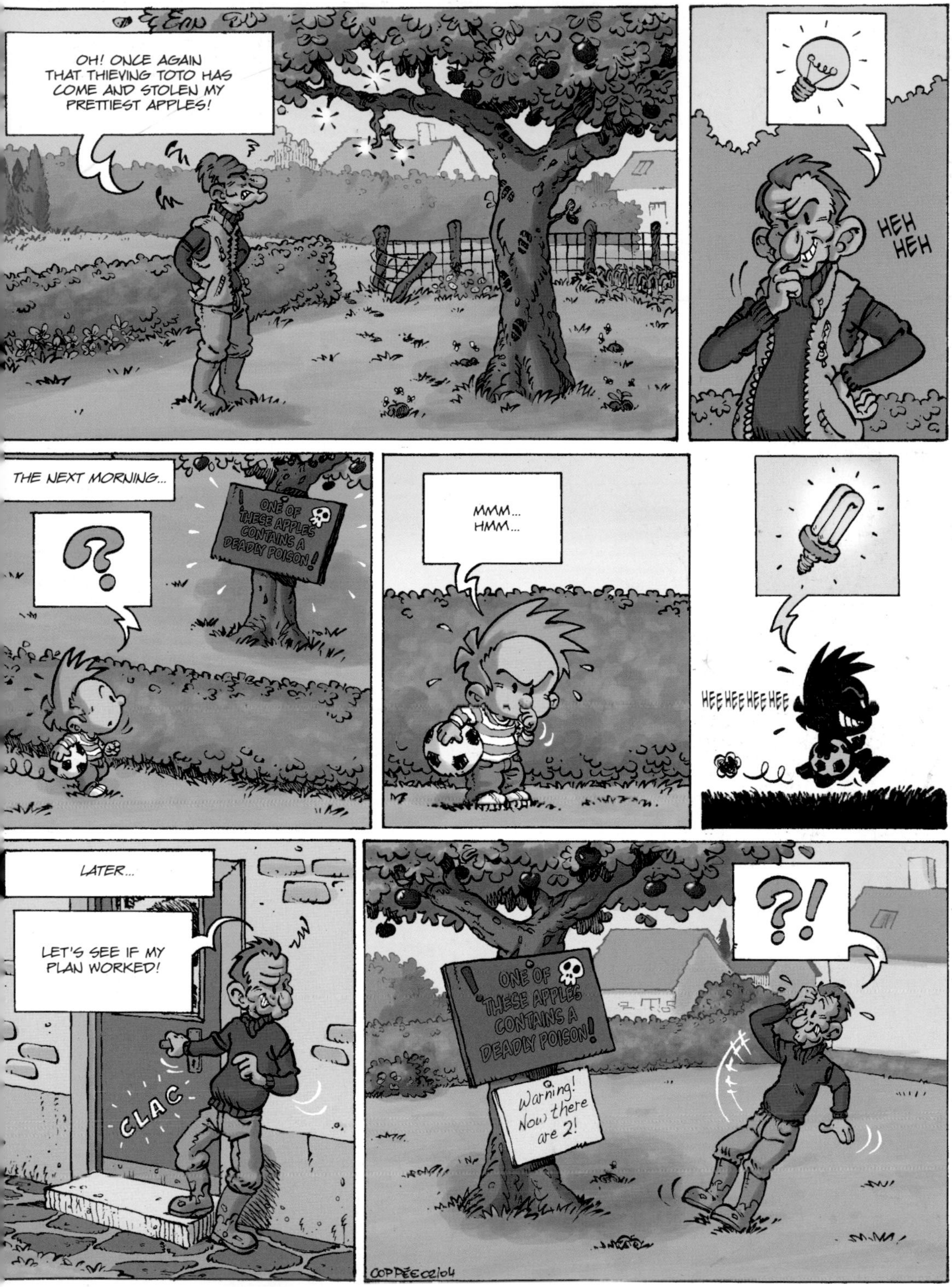

OH! ONCE AGAIN THAT THIEVING TOTO HAS COME AND STOLEN MY PRETTIEST APPLES!
HEH HEH
THE NEXT MORNING...
?
ONE OF THESE APPLES CONTAINS A DEADLY POISON!
MMM... HMM...
HEE HEE HEE HEE
LATER...
LET'S SEE IF MY PLAN WORKED!
CLAC
ONE OF THESE APPLES CONTAINS A DEADLY POISON!
Warning! Now there are 2!
?!
COPPÉE 02/04

"Who Knows Who It Is?"

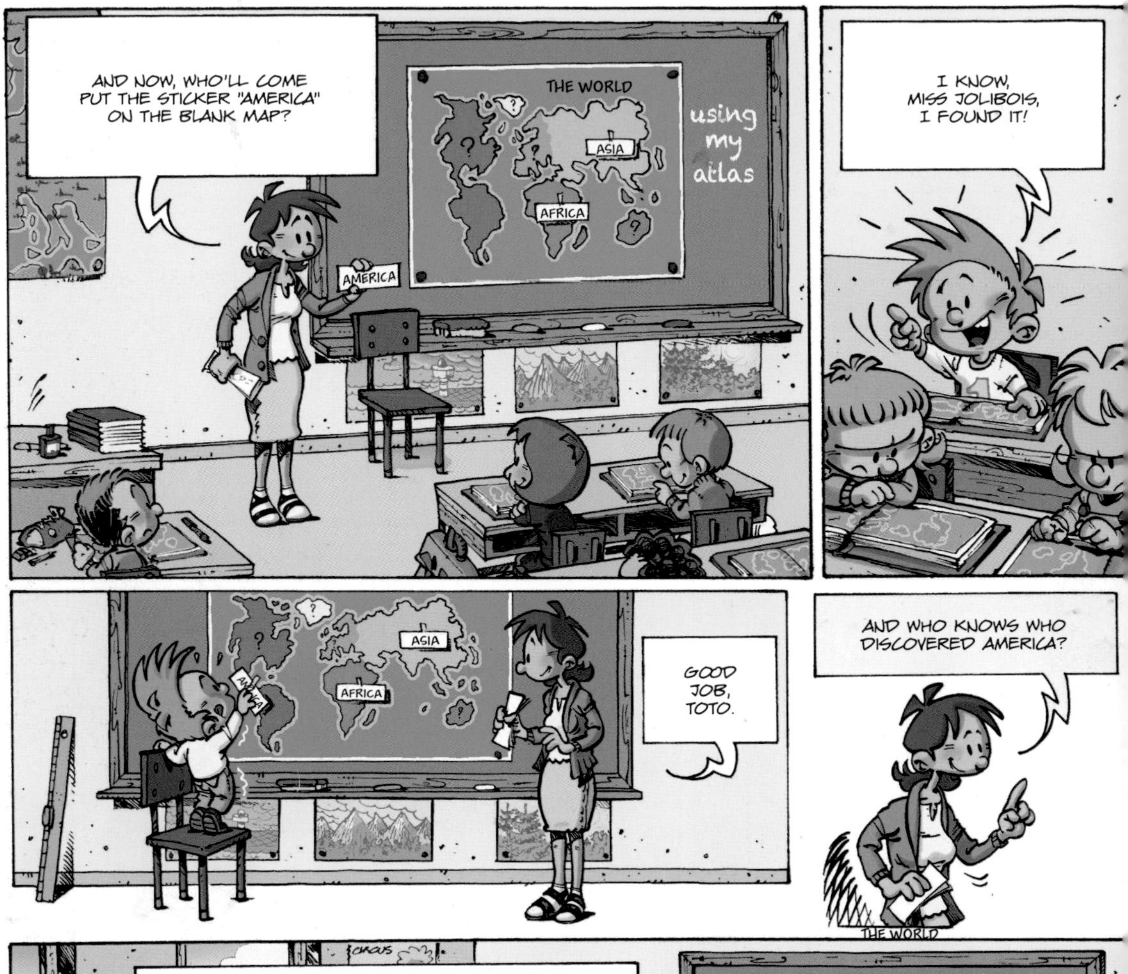
AND NOW, WHO'LL COME PUT THE STICKER "AMERICA" ON THE BLANK MAP?
THE WORLD
ASIA
AFRICA
AMERICA
using my atlas
I KNOW, MISS JOLIBOIS, I FOUND IT!
ASIA
AFRICA
GOOD JOB, TOTO.
AND WHO KNOWS WHO DISCOVERED AMERICA?
THE WORLD
WHY, TOTO DID, MISS JOLIBOIS!
AMERICA
ASIA
AFRICA
using my atlas

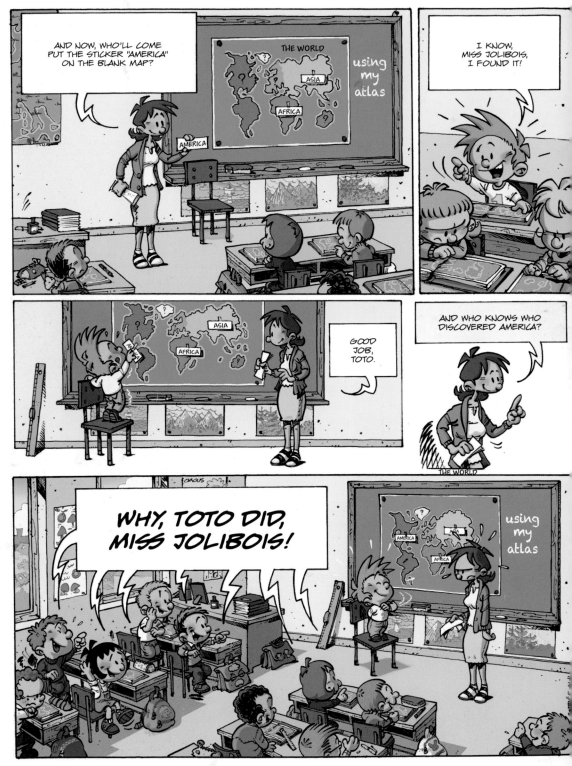

"A Piggish Dinner"

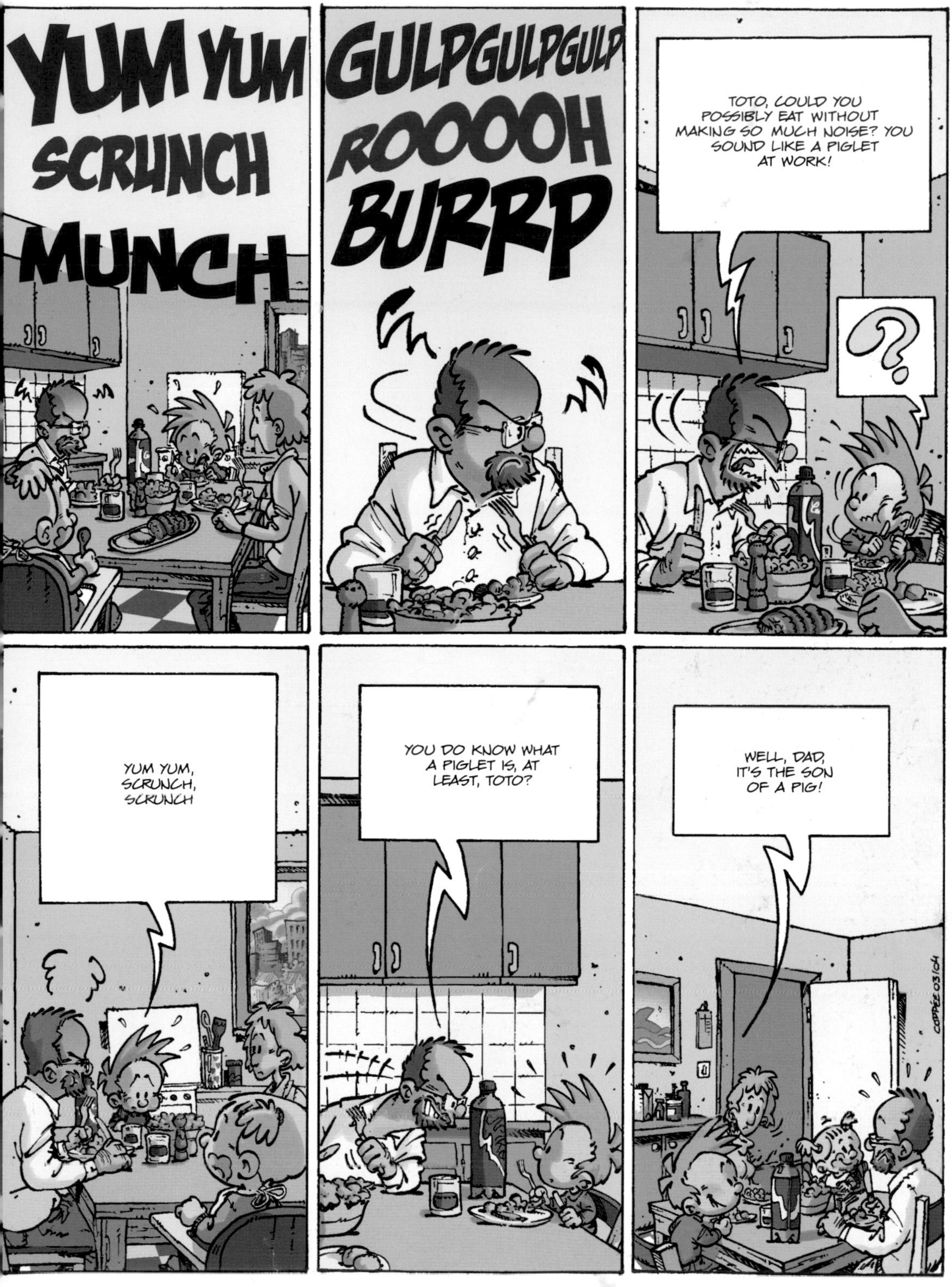
YUM YUM
SCRUNCH
MUNCH
GULPGULPGULP
ROOOOH
BURRP
TOTO, COULD YOU POSSIBLY EAT WITHOUT MAKING SO MUCH NOISE? YOU SOUND LIKE A PIGLET AT WORK!
?
YUM YUM, SCRUNCH, SCRUNCH
YOU DO KNOW WHAT A PIGLET IS, AT LEAST, TOTO?
WELL, DAD, IT'S THE SON OF A PIG!
COPPÉE 03/04

"A Genealogical Zoo"

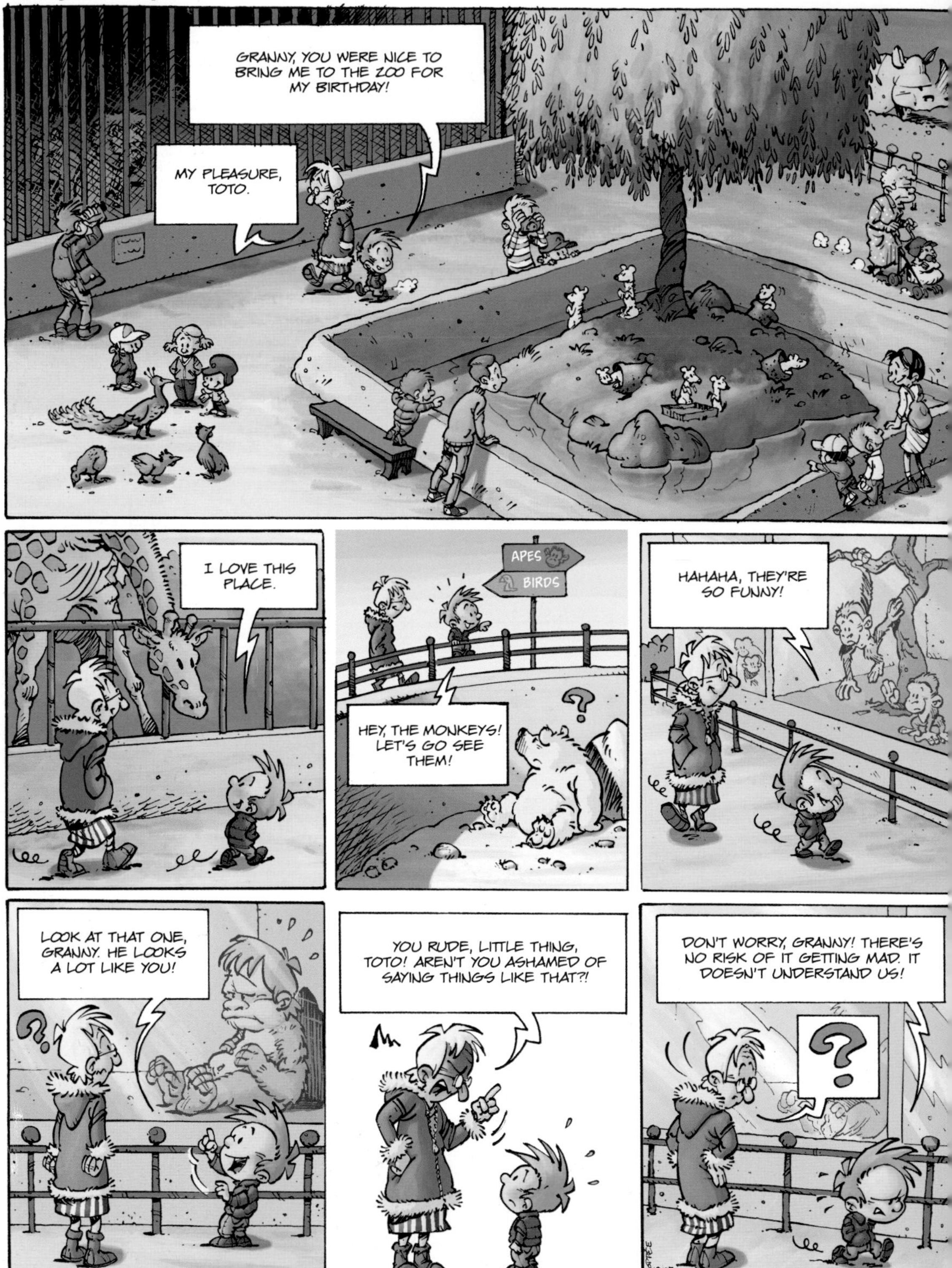
GRANNY, YOU WERE NICE TO BRING ME TO THE ZOO FOR MY BIRTHDAY!
MY PLEASURE, TOTO.
I LOVE THIS PLACE.
APES
BIRDS
HEY, THE MONKEYS! LET'S GO SEE THEM!
HAHAHA, THEY'RE SO FUNNY!
LOOK AT THAT ONE, GRANNY. HE LOOKS A LOT LIKE YOU!
YOU RUDE, LITTLE THING, TOTO! AREN'T YOU ASHAMED OF SAYING THINGS LIKE THAT?!
DON'T WORRY, GRANNY! THERE'S NO RISK OF IT GETTING MAD. IT DOESN'T UNDERSTAND US!

"A Funny Fall"

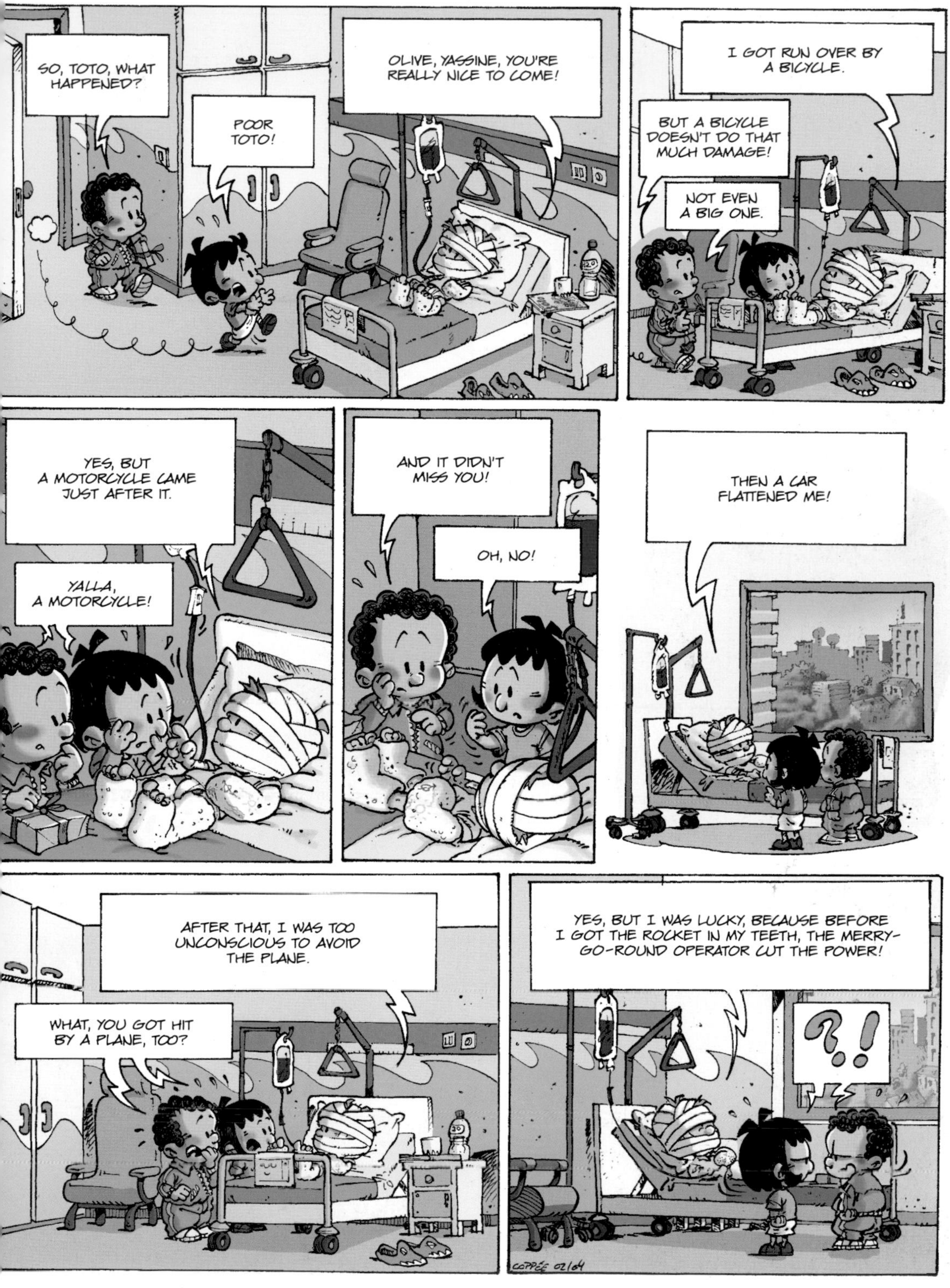
SO, TOTO, WHAT HAPPENED?
POOR TOTO!
OLIVE, YASSINE, YOU'RE REALLY NICE TO COME!
I GOT RUN OVER BY A BICYCLE.
BUT A BICYCLE DOESN'T DO THAT MUCH DAMAGE!
NOT EVEN A BIG ONE.
YES, BUT A MOTORCYCLE CAME JUST AFTER IT.
YALLA, A MOTORCYCLE!
AND IT DIDN'T MISS YOU!
OH, NO!
THEN A CAR FLATTENED ME!
AFTER THAT, I WAS TOO UNCONSCIOUS TO AVOID THE PLANE.
WHAT, YOU GOT HIT BY A PLANE, TOO?
YES, BUT I WAS LUCKY, BECAUSE BEFORE I GOT THE ROCKET IN MY TEETH, THE MERRY-GO-ROUND OPERATOR CUT THE POWER!
?!
COPPÉE 02/04

"Slow Times"

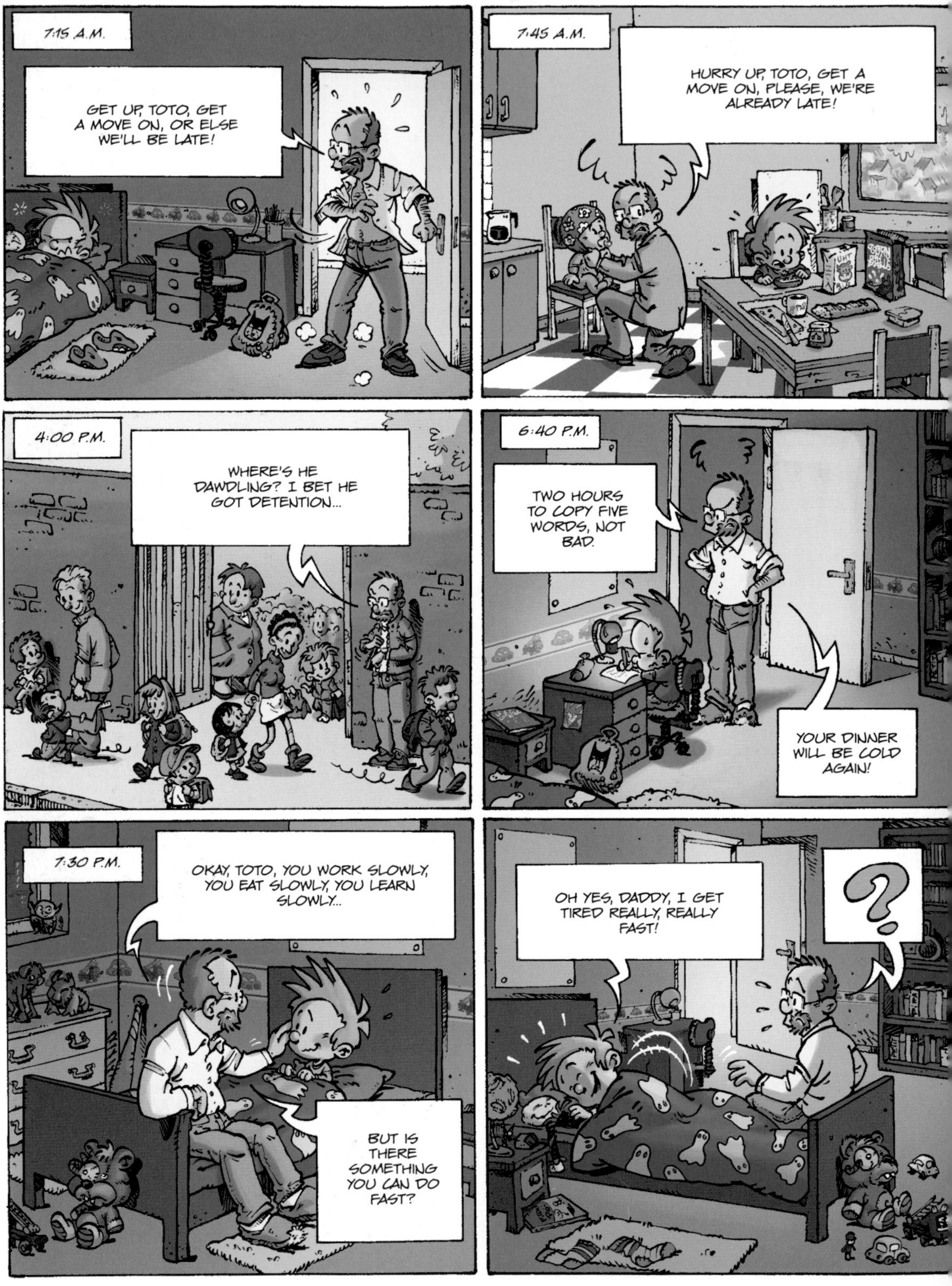
7:15 A.M.
GET UP, TOTO, GET A MOVE ON, OR ELSE WE'LL BE LATE!
7:45 A.M.
HURRY UP, TOTO, GET A MOVE ON, PLEASE, WE'RE ALREADY LATE!
4:00 P.M.
WHERE'S HE DAWDLING? I BET HE GOT DETENTION...
6:40 P.M.
TWO HOURS TO COPY FIVE WORDS, NOT BAD.
YOUR DINNER WILL BE COLD AGAIN!
7:30 P.M.
OKAY, TOTO, YOU WORK SLOWLY, YOU EAT SLOWLY, YOU LEARN SLOWLY...
BUT IS THERE SOMETHING YOU CAN DO FAST?
OH YES, DADDY, I GET TIRED REALLY, REALLY FAST!
?

"The Fruit of Fractions"

"*Anxiety*"

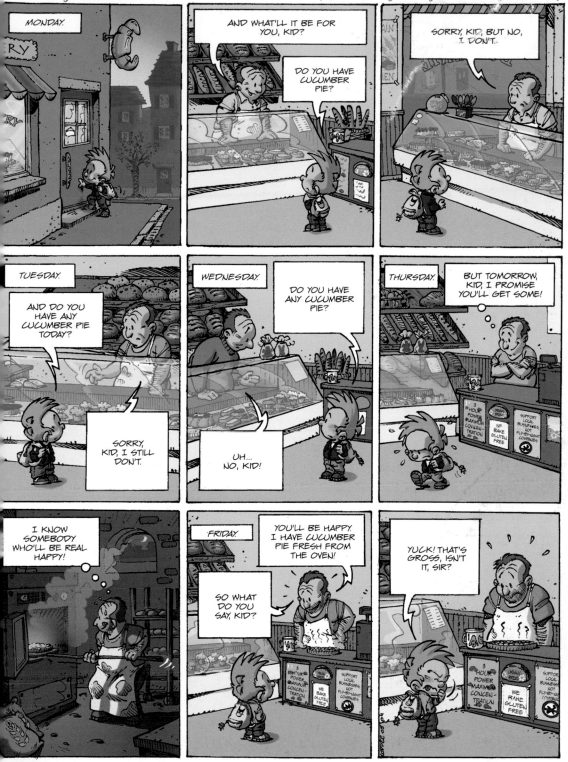

"Sacred Cows"

"H2 Uh-Oh!"

"Service Charges"

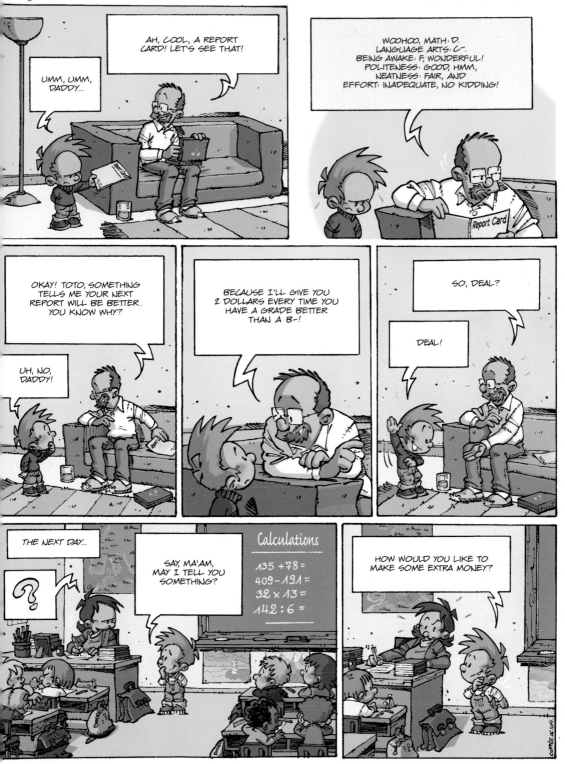

"Observation Skills"

WATCH OUT FOR PAPERCUTZ

Welcome to the fun-filled, formerly-French, first TOTO TROUBLE graphic novel by Thierry Coppée from Papercutz, the petite comics company dedicated to publishing great graphic novels for all ages. I'm Jim Salicrup, the Editor-in-Chief at Papercutz and substitute teacher at Toto's school.

We're thrilled to add TOTO TROUBLE to our ever-expanding line-up of graphic novels. We're big fans of little Toto, and we hope you enjoy his jokes as much as we do. In fact, this series was originally published in France and called "*Les Blagues de Toto*," which is "Toto's Jokes." We changed the name of the series to TOTO TROUBLE to tie-in to the animated series featuring Toto that ran on the Starz channel, but if you blinked, you probably missed it.

Fortunately, you didn't need to watch the TV show, to enjoy TOTO TROUBLE. In fact, to even further enhance your enjoyment of TOTO TROUBLE we've come up with a scorecard (Bet you thought we were kidding on the back cover!) for you to keep track of the jokes in this occasionally gross and goofy graphic novel. Now it gets a little tricky sometimes—believe me, I've tried it—but the goal here is to use Roman numerals to keep track of how many of the various type of jokes are in this volume.

Dad Jokes	
Dead Cat Jokes	
Dead Dog Jokes	
Dead Goldfish Jokes	
Dumb Student Jokes	
Eating-a-Slug Jokes	
Poop (No Joke, Just Poop)	
Poop Jokes	
Teacher Jokes	
Toto-is-Dumb Jokes	
Tricking-Mom Jokes	
Tricking School Jokes	
Wee-Wee Jokes	

You may have noticed on some pages, five to be precise, various people are awarded prizes for jokes. These are the winning entries in a joke competition held in France, where amongst the prizes, the winning jokes got to be published in *Les Blagues de Toto* and illustrated by Thierry Coppée himself (We'll have a photo and bio of Toto's creator in TOTO TROUBLE #2!) What do you think of having a joke competition like that here in TOTO TROUBLE? Let us know by contacting us by the various means listed below. You can also tell us what you thought of TOTO TROUBLE #1 "Back to Crass." If you liked it, feel free to post or tweet about TOTO TROUBLE online. And don't forget to look for TOTO TROUBLE #2 "A Deadly Jokester" coming soon to the bookstore nearest you!

So until next time, be sure to stay out of trouble!

Thanks,

Jim

STAY IN TOUCH!

EMAIL: salicrup@papercutz.com
WEB: papercutz.com
TWITTER: @papercutzgn
FACEBOOK: PAPERCUTZGRAPHICNOVELS
MAIL: Papercutz, 160 Broadway, Suite 700,
East Wing, New York, NY 10038

More Great Graphic Novels from PAPERCUTZ™

DINOSAURS #2
"Bite of the Albertosaurus"
Science facts combined with Dino-humor!

ERNEST & REBECCA #4
"The Land of Walking Stones"
A 6 ½ year old girl and her microbial buddy against the world!

THE GARFIELD SHOW #3
"Long Lost Lyman"
As seen on the Cartoon Network!

BENNY BREAKIRON #4
"Uncle Placid"
Benny helps his Uncle protect the finance minister of Fürengrootsbadenschtein from all kinds of dangerous danger!

THE SMURFS #17
"The Strange Awakening of Lazy Smurf"
Has Lazy Smurf been asleep for 200 years?

LEGO® NINJAGO #9
"Night of the Nindroids"
Will Zane betray his friends? Plus, an all-new Green Ninja Story!

Available at better booksellers everywhere!

Or order directly from us! DINOSAURS is available in hardcover only for $10.99; ERNEST & REBECCA is $11.99 in hardcover only; THE GARFIELD SHOW is available in paperback for $7.99, in hardcover for $11.99; BENNY BREAKIRON is available in hardcover only for $11.99; THE SMURFS are available in paperback for $5.99, in hardcover for $10.99; and LEGO NINJAGO is available in paperback for $6.99 and hardcover for $10.99.

Please add $4.00 for postage and handling for the first book, add $1.00 for each additional book.

Please make check payable to NBM Publishing. Send to: PAPERCUTZ, 160 Broadway, Suite 700, East Wing, New York, NY 10038
(1-800-886-1223)